ARMSTRONG'S WAR

Badger Armstrong, alias Quick Jim Butler, rode home to Texas to make peace with his family. Fifteen years earlier he'd walked out, swearing he'd never return . . . Mort Quarry had acquired all the best grazing land in Deaf Smith County — except for the Double-A-Slash Ranch run by Badger's father, Bale Armstrong. But with his brother on Quarry's payroll, he rides into trouble. In the war against Quarry, Badger will have to survive both his father's wrath and the bullets of his brother.

LEE PIERCE

---◆---

ARMSTRONG'S WAR

Complete and Unabridged

LINFORD
Leicester

First published in Great Britain in 2005 by
Robert Hale Limited
London

First Linford Edition
published 2006
by arrangement with
Robert Hale Limited
London

British Library CIP Data

Pierce, Lee
    Armstrong's war.—Large print ed.—
Linford western library
1. Western stories
2. Large type books
I. Title
823.9'2 [F]

ISBN 1–84617–436–8

Published by
F. A. Thorpe (Publishing)
Anstey, Leicestershire

Set by Words & Graphics Ltd.
Anstey, Leicestershire
Printed and bound in Great Britain by
T. J. International Ltd., Padstow, Cornwall

This book is printed on acid-free paper

1

The crack of a pistol shot shattered the morning silence. Jim Butler jerked his mount to a halt, his hand dropping to his six-gun. He was high atop a rocky ridge that overlooked a long sandy arroyo. The shot had come from below. Dismounting, he hunkered down and trotted towards the edge of the ridge. A few feet from the rim, he dropped to his belly and crawled the rest of the way. Peering over the precipice, he frowned at what he saw.

Four cowboys with pistols drawn sat horseback on the edge of the arroyo. Three of the riders were men from Jim's past. Below the men, kneeling in the dirt, were four Mexicans and a half butchered longhorn steer. Another Mexican lay on his back; blood oozed from a gunshot wound on his side. Of the four riders, the youngest one with the blond hair was bellowing like he was in charge.

'I told you my daddy was making a big mistake letting them Mexs start farming on our property.'

One of the cowhands, a scruffy looking puncher, nodded in agreement. The other two glanced at each other, saying nothing.

'You're sure 'nuff right about that one, Chris,' said the nodding cowboy, punctuating his statement by launching an enormous glob of stringy tobacco juice that hurtled through the air in the general direction of the Mexicans.

'Señor Armstrong,' said one of the Mexicans, 'We do not kill this cow. It was dead when we found it. The neck was broken, maybe from a fall into this arroyo. We did not want the meat to go bad, so we butchered as much as we could carry to our families. We would have told El Patron when we saw him next. This is *verdad, señor*, the truth, I swear it.'

'Don't lie to me,' said Chris Armstrong. 'You stinking bean eaters ain't worth the spit in my mouth. Get your sorry carcasses into that cart yonder and head out towards our ranch house. When my daddy finds out about this he'll make sure you heathens get to dance on the end of a short rope. I heard you boys love to dance. Ain't that right?'

The scruffy cowboy laughed like he thought his boss had said about the funniest thing he'd ever heard. The other two sat stone faced.

'Say, Chris,' — this coming from the larger of the two silent cowboys, a barrel-chested man with a gray bush of a beard — 'See the way that old steer's neck is all twisted back. That sucker's broke clean. Maybe these fellers are levelling with you?'

'Shank Halsey, how long have you worked for the Double-A-Slash?'

'Chris, you know I was with your daddy when he rode into this country. Shucks, son, I've been here forever.'

'If you want to stay here old man, you had better shut your mouth.'

The last of the riders, a lanky mass of freckles named Rusty Puckett, started to say something, but Shank nudged him, and he backed off.

Jim had known Shank Halsey and Rusty Puckett all of his life, and Chris was his younger brother. Jim started to speak up, but decided to watch some more before committing himself.

'*Señor*,' said the Mexican who had spoken before, 'what about Manuel? We must get him to a doctor. He is bleeding too much. He might die here.'

'Bleed to death or hang, it don't make any difference. He's going to die anyway,' said Chris. 'Didn't I tell you to get in that wagon, Mex? Now, go!' The young firebrand turned to the scruffy rider. 'Val, you make sure these boys get to the house in a hurry. I'm going ahead to tell Bale what we found and to get the ropes ready.'

Not waiting for an answer, Chris Armstrong dug his spurs into his horse and took off at a gallop towards the headquarters of the Double-A-Slash ranch. Seconds later, Shank Halsey headed out in the same direction.

Jim waited until all the men were out of sight, climbed aboard his steel dun mare, and worked his way down the embankment to the arroyo. When he got there the wounded Mexican was still breathing, but the man had lost a lot of blood. Jim rummaged through his saddle-bags until he found a pint bottle of whiskey and a clean shirt. He wrapped the shirt around the wound to staunch the flow of blood. He then gathered up a few pieces of wood and started a small fire. After putting a pot of water on to boil, Jim looked over at the unconscious man. The Mexican farmer's breathing was coming in shallow ragged gulps. Jim had removed more than his share of lead chunks in the last fifteen years, but never from a man this close to death.

'*Amigo*,' said Jim, 'I don't hold much chance of you living through the night, but I'll do my best to fix your wound. Then it'll be up to the man in the sky to decide whether you live or die.'

Jim unsheathed the knife he wore on his belt and placed it by the fire. He cleaned the wound with hot water. Then he poured some of the whiskey over the knife blade. Straddling the still unconscious man, using great care, Jim probed into the bullet hole.

'I think I feel it, *amigo*,' said Jim. He was sweating but not from the heat. He reached the tiny piece of lead and, with a little effort, popped it out.

'You're lucky, pardner,' he said. 'It doesn't look like the bullet hit any vitals.'

Afterwards, he packed the wound and wrapped it with strips torn from his clean shirt.

Jim reckoned he was two hours north of Two Bucks City, Texas. He had planned on reaching the town by early afternoon, but the shooting of this Mexican farmer had altered his plans. He couldn't leave the wounded man and moving him was out of the question. He unsaddled his horse and picketed the big mare over a large patch of green grass. He arranged his gear on the ground and checked on the Mexican. The man's breathing had become more regular since the bullet had been removed. He seemed to be resting.

'*Amigo*,' said Jim, 'you survived my butchering well enough; you just might make it after all. I made camp and I'll stay with you through the night. I can't promise anything beyond that. It's been a coon's age since I had me a fresh beefsteak, so I believe I'll carve me a big ol' hunk of this steer and cook it for my dinner. I'll save some to make a broth for you, if you make it.'

★ ★ ★

Chris Armstrong charged up to the Double-A-Slash ranch house like the devil himself was chasing him. He jumped off of his horse before the

7

animal stopped, bounded onto the porch, and stomped inside.

'Dad,' he hollered, 'Dad, are you here?'

An answer came from the kitchen. Chris entered the room to find his father sitting at the table drinking a cup of coffee. Maria, the Mexican cook, was washing dishes.

'Señor Chris, would you like some coffee?' said Maria. She wiped her hands on her apron and started toward the coffee pot sitting on a potbellied stove in the corner.

Chris ignored the offer and ripped into his father. 'Dad, I told you, letting those greaser farmers squat on our land would cost us. Well, now they have gone and killed a steer and tried to butcher it. I'm going to teach all of those Mexican peons a lesson.'

'Whoa there, Chris,' said Bale Armstrong. The chair under him protested, squeaking loudly, as Bale tried to straighten his bent frame up to face his irate son. 'Calm down. Sit here, get you a cup of coffee, and tell me what's going on. That's a pretty strong accusation you just made. Did you see these Mexicans kill the steer?'

'No, I didn't see them, but they did it. They had already killed it and were butchering it when we got there.'

Maria's slender body stiffened at the accusations. 'Excuse me, Señor Bale, but I must go to the henhouse for a few minutes.' She didn't wait for Bale Armstrong's answer.

Throwing a tattered shawl around her narrow shoulders, the old woman hurried outside. The screen door banged shut behind her. Bale looked up as she left, and then back at his son. His eyes were hard.

Placing both hands on the table, using great effort, Bale pushed himself to a standing position. His worn out legs creaked like rusty hinges as he stood. 'Was anybody with you when you found the steer?'

'Shank and Rusty were with me. Val Rose was there too.'

'Where are they?'

'Bringing in the rustlers. I'm going to hang them. That ought to keep the rest away from Double-A-Slash livestock.'

'Hang 'em! That's a little bit harsh, isn't it?'

'Bale, those greasers have got to learn once and for all who is boss around here.'

Bale looked Chris in the eye. 'You had better not forget who is boss around here, either, Chris. I don't like it when you call me by my first name. It shows disrespect. Ever since you started hanging around with that Quarry bunch, son, you have been making some mighty poor decisions. You know Mort Quarry wants this ranch, and he will stoop to anything to get it.'

Chris opened his mouth but nothing came out. He sat for a moment, and then stood up. 'I don't have time for this. I'm going to the barn for some rope. I've got a bunch of Mexicans to hang.'

Before Chris could go out, Shank

10

Halsey strode into the room. He stood in the doorway blocking Chris's exit. Chris tried to go around him, but Halsey stood his ground.

'Boss, we got to talk, and I'd just as soon Chris be here to listen to what I've got to say.' He shot a withering glance towards the younger Armstrong. Chris backed up against the cabinet and stood silent.

'I'm sure you already got the story from Chris, boss, but I want to make sure he didn't leave nothin' out.'

Bale Armstrong looked at Chris and back at Shank. He cocked his head to the side and motioned for the old wrangler to continue.

'Boss, them farmers was butcherin' that steer when we came up on 'em. The dumb thing was in the arroyo with its neck all twisted back. They said they found it there with a broke neck, and they was just tryin' to save some of the meat. One of 'em said he was goin' to tell you, next time he saw you.'

'Is this true, Chris?' said Bale,

narrowing his brow.

'They said that, but everybody knows a Mex would rather tell a lie than eat tortillas and chilli peppers.'

'That ain't all, Boss,' said Shank, in a low voice. 'Chris shot one of 'em. The feller didn't have no gun, either.'

'Good Lord, Chris,' said Bale, his face blanching white. 'You shot an unarmed man?'

'Come on, Dad, it was a stinking Mexican.'

'Is the man dead?'

'Don't know boss; Chris made us leave him there and bring the rest of 'em here to hang.'

'Where are the rest of the men who were doing the butchering, Shank?'

'Rusty and Valentine are bringin' 'em in. They ought to be here any minute, now.'

'Shank you get Maria to take a wagon, and you two hightail it back to the arroyo. If that man is still alive, bring him back here.'

Bale Armstrong turned to his youngest son. 'Chris, you tell the boys to let those Mexicans go and tell Rusty to escort them back to their homes. I'll go out there tomorrow and apologize to them. And boy, you had better hope that man you shot isn't dead.'

Chris looked at his father, disbelief covering his face. 'You tell them Bale. I'm done working here. Mort Quarry offered me a job, and I'm going to take it. He knows how to treat his men, and he always needs another gun.' He turned toward the door. 'Get out of my way Shank, or you'll be the next man I shoot.'

Shank stepped aside, and Chris stormed out of the kitchen. Shank looked down at his boss and old friend. 'He'll come back, Bale. He just ain't quite growed up yet. Maybe him bein' away for a while might help, it sure can't hurt. I'll get one of the hands to hitch up a wagon, and, on our way out, I'll tell Rusty what to do with them farmer fellers.'

Shank headed for the front door. Bale Armstrong dropped into his chair and bowed his head.

2

Jim was moving to check on the wounded man when the clatter of an approaching wagon caught his attention. Standing up, he loosened the thong on his .44, and stood relaxed, as the wagon pulled up to the edge of the arroyo. Jim was surprised to see a woman driving the rig. Shank Halsey rode beside the wagon. As the woman pulled the team of horses to a stop, the big puncher reined his horse in to her left.

'Howdy,' said Jim, 'sit and rest a spell, coffee's hot.'

'*Gracias, señor*,' said the lady.

'*Usted son Mexicana?*' said Jim.

'Yes, I am, but I speak English.'

'Good,' said Jim. 'Maybe you can help me, *señorita*. There is a Mexican man here. He has been shot. I took the bullet out and did my best to help him, but I don't know if he will live or not.'

Maria hopped down from the wagon seat and scurried over to the wounded man.

'It is Manuel, *por Dios*, he is alive.'

Shank glared down at Jim. 'I know you from somewhere?' he said. 'What's your name?'

'Most folks call me Jim Butler. What's your handle?'

'It don't matter who I am. What's your interest in this hurt feller?'

'No special interest, I was just ridin' by, looked down into this arroyo and noticed the steer. When I rode down, I saw the wounded man. The rest you know.'

'You had a fire. Did you cook up some of that animal?'

'Well, him being dead and all, just wasting away, yes sir, I did have me a big chunk of beef. It sure was good, too.'

'You're on Double-A-Slash land, feller. That steer belongs to Bale Armstrong.'

'He must be the big 'he coon' around here then.'

'Has been for thirty years and will be for another thirty.' Shank said. 'You the Jim Butler who was involved in that little ruckus up in Oklahoma about a year ago?'

'Yep, that's me.'

'You got yourself a reputation, Butler. We don't need no more two-bit gunfighters around these parts. You saddle up and shuck it for somewheres else.'

Jim smiled at the old cowpoke. 'You people sure ain't too friendly around here, *amigo*.'

Before the conversation could heat up anymore, Maria called out. 'You two quit wasting time and help me get Manuel into the wagon.'

Jim looked at Shank, winked and turned to help Maria with Manuel. Shank sat his horse, his hand resting on the butt of his six-gun and watched.

With the wounded man loaded and settled in as best could be expected,

Maria clicked her tongue and the horses started off toward the ranch headquarters. Shank stayed behind with his eyes on Jim, until the wagon was thirty feet away. He started to turn his horse to follow, when Jim spoke.

'Shank, hold up a minute. I want to talk to you.'

Shank Halsey stopped cold. Turning his horse back around, he rode to within spitting distance of Jim. There was a puzzled look on his face.

'How come you know my name, Butler? Where'd we cross trails?'

'Shoot, Marion Charles Halsey, why shouldn't I know your name, you old mossy horn.'

Shank jerked back almost falling off his horse. 'Ain't nobody around these parts knows my Christian name. Who are you?'

'Get down off that hay burner, and have a cup of Arbuckle's with me. The coffee has been on the fire for a couple of hours so it ought to be just the way you like it.'

Jim dug a tin cup out of his saddlebags, filled it with the strong hot brew, and handed it to the big cowboy. He took off his hat and ran a rough hand through his bushy hair. 'I'm Bale Armstrong Jr., Shank,' Jim said. 'I've come back from the dead.'

Shank's face turned to chalk. The tin cup dropped from his limp fingers and clattered across the hard-scrabble ground. He stood motionless staring into the cobalt blue eyes of Jim Butler. 'By the Lord Almighty, you are Bale Armstrong Jr . . . Badger, it's you!'

'Nobody's called me Badger in fifteen years. It sounds strange, but it sounds pretty good. How are you, old *compadre*?'

Jim Butler stuck out his right hand, and Shank grabbed it, jerking it like a pump handle. Both men briefly embraced, and then backed off. Shank kept on shaking his head.

'Doggone it, Badger, the old man told us you was dead; it was nine or ten years ago. He said you got killed in some sort of gunfight down Arizona way. Why, he even went down there to see your grave. What in tarnation happened?'

Jim smoothed out his hair and put his hat back on. 'Let's get over yonder next to the fire, and I'll tell you a little bit about it.'

They hunkered down, and Jim began his story.

'When Poppa kicked me off the ranch, I drifted south into Mexico, and ended up throwin' in with some rough *hombres*. We ran cattle back and forth across the border and raised cain on both sides. One night in Tombstone, one of the gang came out second best in a disagreement with Doc Holliday.'

'Holliday kill him?' asked Shank.

'Yep, that's when I got the idea.'

'Idea for what?'

'Back then, I was still mad at my father. I had some papers on me that said who I was, and when nobody was looking, I slipped them inside the dead man's coat. The undertaker buried Bale

Armstrong Jr. the next day. I took the name Jim Butler after James Butler Hickok, 'Wild Bill', and that's what I've gone by ever since.'

Jim got up and stretched his legs. He took his hat off and raked fingers through his hair. Telling his story to Shank had brought back unsettling memories.

'By durn, Badger,' said Shank, rising to his feet, 'everybody knows about Quick Jim Butler. Some say you're the fastest man with a handgun that there is. I heard you killed over a hundred men. Is that right, Badger?'

'No it ain't right, Shank. I've killed some men, but only when there was no other choice. I hope I'm through with killing. That's one of the reasons I came back home. I want to settle down on the ranch, if my father will let me.'

'Say, Badger, we got to get on back to the ranch and tell Bale you're alive. Man, I can't hardly wait to see the look on Rusty's ol' freckled face when he hears the news.'

20

'No, Shank, I don't want anyone else to know I'm back, at least, not yet. I was up on that ridge yonder, and I saw what happened with those Mexicans. Something's not right.'

'Badger, it's that dad gum Mort Quarry and his bunch. They're tryin' to get your daddy's ranch, and they don't pay no never mind how they do it. Quarry owns most of Two Bucks City already but that ain't enough for a greedy crook like him. He wants it all.'

'Shank, what happened to Chris? He shot that man for no reason. Since when has it been a crime to butcher an animal that was already dead?'

'Aw, Badger, over the last year, Chris has turned into somebody I don't know any more. He's been hangin' out with that Quarry gang, and not hardly doin' anything to help on the ranch. A little while ago, he told Bale he was quittin' the Double-A-Slash because Bale wouldn't let him hang them farmers.'

Jim rubbed his hand down his mustache. 'Shank, I'm going to ride into Two Bucks City tomorrow as Jim Butler. I don't want anyone else to know who I am. As far as I'm concerned, right now, Badger Armstrong died in Tombstone. I'll let it be known who I am when I'm ready.'

'Whatever you say, Boss.'

Jim raised his eyes upon hearing the word 'boss'. Shank Halsey was grinning like a possum full of paw paws.

Shank stayed on for awhile talking to Jim about what was going on in Deaf Smith County. The more he heard, the more Jim became concerned he had arrived home too late to save the family ranch. Bale Armstrong Jr. might have died in Tombstone, but Quick Jim Butler was alive and well, and he intended to turn over every rock in the Two Bucks country until he found the right snake to stomp on.

3

The sun was a glaring yellow orb staring out of a cloudless Texas sky when Jim Butler rode into Two Bucks City. Recent spring rains had turned the panhandle country green. Swathes of orange, red, blue, and yellow flowers shot up everywhere, gracing the landscape with a rainbow of colors. In spite of the trepidation Jim was feeling about coming back after so many years away, he felt good.

The first thing he did was look for the telegraph office. He was surprised to find it in the same old building. Dismounting, he tied the mare to a rail and stepped inside the office. The place reeked of rotting wood. Buckets had been placed at various spots on the floor to catch rain from a leaky roof. A telegrapher sat behind a scarred wooden desk in the far corner. He did not look up when Jim entered the building.

'I need to send a telegram,' Jim said in a soft voice.

'Paper and pen's on the table. If you can't write, it will cost you a nickel for me to scribble it out for you.' The young man never looked up.

'I can write *amigo*. Can you read?'

''Course, I can read,' the man said, looking up at Jim. A piercing black stare greeted him, and his lips froze in place.

'Pardon me, sir.' The telegrapher's voice squeaked like a trapped mouse. 'I meant no disrespect.'

Jim wrote out his telegram and handed it to the man. 'How much?' He said, reaching into his pocket for change.

The man read the telegram and looked up. 'Do you work for Mr Quarry, sir?'

'What if I do?'

'There would be no charge to send this telegram.'

'In that case, I do work for the man. Where could I find him right now?'

'Mr Quarry could be anywhere, sir. He owns almost all of the town. Dude Miller is usually in the Golden Ace saloon this time of day.'

'Who is Dude Miller?'

'Why, he's Mr Quarry's foreman. I thought you said you worked for them? If you don't, you will have to pay for this telegram.'

Jim stared at the telegrapher until the man lowered his eyes. 'You calling me a liar?'

'No, sir, I just thought . . . '

Jim took a step closer to the man. 'Send the telegram.'

'Yes sir.'

The man was pounding the telegraph key when Jim stepped back out on the sidewalk. As he walked up the street, Jim saw the Golden Ace two blocks down the way and across; he turned and headed in that direction. Before he reached the saloon, Jim noticed the bank half a block away and veered off towards the native stone building. The sign above the entrance said Deaf

Smith County Bank; underneath read M. Quarry, Pres. Jim stepped inside and felt instant relief from the pounding Texas sun. A young woman behind the teller's cage had her back to him. She seemed oblivious to his presence. Jim put his hand to his mouth and coughed twice. The young lady gave a start and whirled around.

'Pardon me sir,' she said. 'I didn't hear you come in. May I help you?'

Two shimmering emerald eyes, a petite upturned nose, and a perfect pair of cherry lips in a flawless oval face combined to strip Jim of his powers of communication.

'Sir, sir, are you OK?'

'Uh, yes, ma'am, I think so.'

'You look like you've seen a ghost.'

'No, ma'am, just the prettiest girl I have ever seen in my life.' Jim Butler was never one to mince words.

The young lady blushed, and Jim thought how she looked like a pink prairie rose, all fresh right after the dew had fallen.

'I'm sorry, ma'am. I need to transfer some money to this bank from the Territorial Bank of New Mexico in Albuquerque.'

'How much would you like to transfer, sir?'

Jim told her and after receiving the proper information she wrote up the transfer document and handed it to Jim to sign.

'May I help you with something else, Mr Butler?'

'No, ma'am, I believe that will do it.'

'It's not ma'am, Mr Butler, it's Miss, Miss Melinda Quarry.'

'Yes, miss, I guess it's my Texas upbringing that causes me to address all ladies as ma'am.'

'Please don't apologize, Mr Butler. Gentlemen are scarce out here on the prairie. I appreciate your manners. Are you going to be long in Two Bucks City?'

'That depends on a lot of things, Miss Quarry. If there is enough to hold me here, I might just stay for awhile.'

'Let's hope you decide to stay. My father has big plans for our little town. Opportunities abound for the right men. We will someday be as big and beautiful as Fort Worth or even Dallas.'

'I don't know about the getting bigger part, Miss Quarry, but from where I stand, Two Bucks City has already got both those towns beat in the beauty department. Good afternoon.'

Jim walked out into the sunshine, leaving Melinda Quarry again blushing like a rose. He ambled down to the Golden Ace saloon and stood at the swinging doors letting his eyes grow accustomed to the dim interior light. Satisfied with what he saw, he strode inside.

The place looked like a thousand others Jim had seen. A hardwood bar stood out from one wall with a long gilded mirror hanging behind the bar. A few tables were scattered about and a faro table stood idle in a far corner.

Four cowboys sat at a corner table playing penny ante draw poker. One man stood drinking a beer at the far end of the bar. He wore a brace of pistols cinched up high around his waist. Instead of pointing down as was common, the two holsters pointed inwards towards the man's belt buckle. Jim pegged this one as a gunfighter; one who considered himself an important man in these parts.

'Is your beer cold?' Jim said to the string bean bartender.

'Coldest in town,' said the barkeep, who was almost seven feet tall and skinny as a green twig. The man had a perpetual smile on his homely features. He drew a tall mug of draft and handed it to Jim. Jim chugged every bit of the cool amber liquid and slammed the empty mug down with a loud thunk. The gunman at the end of the bar jerked his head in Jim's direction.

' 'Scuse me there, fella,' said Jim, 'It's just that I haven't had a cold beer in about a week and that one tasted mighty good. Can I buy you a mug, *amigo*?'

The man stared at Jim for a moment, and then went back to his drinking. Jim took off his hat and ran his fingers through his hair. He glanced at the bartender, who motioned for Jim to lean over the bar. Jim turned an ear in the barkeep's direction.

'Mister, you're new here, so maybe you don't know,' said String Bean.

'Don't know what?'

'That feller yonder is Dude Miller. He's the ramrod for Mort Quarry, the most powerful man in these parts. Dude's a curly wolf with his short guns or his fists. He's best left alone. The man's been drinkin' in here all mornin', and he's festerin' up for a fight. I was you, I'd leave him be.'

'What's your name?' asked Jim.

'Most folks call me Stretch. That'll do, I reckon.'

'Stretch, I appreciate the warning, but, with all due respect, you're not me.'

Hat in hand, Jim sidled up to the bad man. 'Say, there, pardner,' he said, 'I reckon you didn't hear me offer you a beer.'

Dude Miller spun towards Jim, his right hand streaking for his pistol. As the gun came up, Jim knocked it away with his hat and smashed a straight right hand that splattered the man's nose. Miller staggered back and Jim bore in on him throwing left hooks and right crosses to the rib cage. Miller tried to fight back, but his feeble efforts were useless, as Jim pounded him into unconsciousness.

Jim Butler stepped back and let Miller slide to the floor. The card players had stood up at the beginning of the fight, and three of them were now muttering amongst themselves; the fourth one was nowhere to be seen. Jim picked up his hat and took a deep breath. He put the hat back on his head and was turning to leave when a human blur careened in through the swinging doors. The blur, Chris Armstrong, stopped long enough to get his bearings. Seeing Dude Miller lying crumpled on the floor, and a stranger standing close to him, Chris dropped his hand, and let it hover over his six-gun.

'You the one who shot Dude?' said Chris. He was trembling.

Stretch, the bartender, flipped a sawed off Greener shotgun out and laid it on the bar. 'There ain't gonna be no shootin' in this saloon, boys. That's the rule and, by heaven, I intend to enforce it.' He turned his attention to Chris Armstrong. 'Chris, you ain't under your daddy's protection anymore, now that you're ridin' for the Quarry brand. You take Dude out of here and go get him fixed up at Doc Whithers. He ain't been shot, just beat up. He started it, and if Mort Quarry asks me, I'll tell him the truth. You know he likes his boys to behave proper here in town. Now, a couple of you hands help Chris get Dude out of here.'

All three of the card players rushed over and picked up the battered man and hauled him outside. The fourth man, who had run for Chris, was Charlie Pratt. He followed along after the other three, muttering to himself.

Chris Armstrong still had his eyes set on Jim Butler.

'Chris,' said Stretch, 'I said get out. Besides, son, on your best day, you couldn't beat this man. He's Jim Butler. I was tendin' bar in Nogales when this feller and Jesus Campo Santos shot it out with the four Carlyle brothers. Now there's just one of them Carlyles left and he ain't got but one good arm. Butler's way too salty for the likes of you, kid. Beat it.'

Chris looked at Jim Butler and spat on the floor at Jim's feet. 'Another day, Butler,' he said. Chris backed out the saloon doors and took off at a trot towards the Doc's.

Stretch watched Chris leave and then he put away his shotgun. He stuck another beer in front of Jim. When Jim started to protest, Stretch raised both hands in front of his face and shook his head. 'You were right, friend,' he said, wiping his brow. 'I ain't you. And I durn sure don't want to be.'

4

The sign on the red brick building read 'Quarry Land and Cattle Company'. Charlie Pratt burst in the front entrance and bee-lined it to a large ornate oak door in the back. He knocked and went in without waiting for an answer.

'Lordy, Mr Quarry, we got us a big problem,' he said, yanking his hat off.

The huge square man, sitting behind an oak desk that matched the door in opulence, looked up at this intruder and frowned. The oversized leather chair moaned as the man lifted his enormous body out of it. Moving with remarkable grace for a man his size, Mort Quarry paced over to the cowboy. His right hand streaked out and grasped the man by the throat, lifting him up on his tip toes. Charlie Pratt's eyes bulged out and his face turned blue.

Mort Quarry stuck his face up next to Pratt's. 'Pratt, if you barge into my office again without being invited, I will choke you to death. If you understand me, nod your head.'

Pratt complied.

Quarry dropped him, strode back behind his desk and sat down. 'Now, Mr Pratt, what is all the ruckus about?'

Charlie Pratt gripped his throat and gagged. Tears rolled down his face as he struggled to breathe. When he gained enough control to speak, his voice screeched like a dying bullfrog.

'Mr Quarry, we have a big problem.'

'You said that already, Charlie. Only problem you have right now is that there had better be a real good reason for you disturbing me today? Now, spit it out.'

'Yes sir, Mr Quarry. There was a fight over at the Golden Ace. Some drifter beat the daylights out of Dude Miller. Three of the boys done toted him to the doc's to get fixed up. But that ain't all, sir. That Armstrong kid tried to call the stranger out, but the feller wouldn't have none of it.'

'What did the new man look like?'

'He was a big one, big as Dude, and quick. I ain't never seen a man throw punches like that. Two minutes, tops, and he had Dude out on the floor.'

'Anybody get his name?'

'Yes sir, the barkeep seemed to know him, called him Jim Butler.'

Mort Quarry's change of attitude was imperceptible to the human eye. 'Where is this Butler now?'

'I reckon he's still in the saloon, leastways, he was when we left.'

Searching through his breast pocket, Quarry came up with a Silver Eagle and pitched it to Charlie. 'You have been very helpful Charlie. I appreciate your coming straight to me. I want you to keep this just between us. Do you understand?'

'Yes sir,' said the lackey, backing out the door and shuffling to the street.

Quarry leaned back in his desk chair, and pondered this new state of affairs.

Jim Butler was a gunman, as dangerous as they come. It was apparent Dude Miller was no match for the man. He had to find out fast if Butler had been hired by Bale Armstrong, or, by some coincidence, was just passing through. Mort Quarry didn't believe in coincidences. He had a hunch something was up. He had to get a note to his man on the inside of Armstrong's camp, and he had to do it pronto.

★　★　★

Jim Butler rode out of Two Bucks City heading for his father's ranch. He had poked the hornet's nest today and started the nasty little boogers to buzz around a bit. The first step in his plan to stop Mort Quarry from stealing the Double-A-Slash had been put into action.

Jim intended to keep his identity a secret for the time being. Shank knew, but he wouldn't tell anyone. Jim rode onto the ranch and angled his horse toward the eastern part where Panther Creek cut across it. Shank had told him that was where the Mexican farmers were settled in. He had said Bale Armstrong gave the farmers permission to live and raise crops on part of the Double-A-Slash. In return the Mexicans were to clean out the brush and diseased trees on the north-eastern part of the ranch.

Jim knew why Mort Quarry wanted his family's ranch. The person who ran the Double-A-Slash controlled the best water in four counties. Water was like gold in the dry Texas panhandle country. He also knew Bale Armstrong would fight with all he had, but his father was seventy years old, maybe older. Shank had told Jim the ranch crew would stand with Bale, but, outside of Shank and Rusty, none of them were gun handy.

The thing that worried Jim the most was his brother. Chris had always been Bale's favorite, and as far as Jim knew, Chris worshipped the old man. He had seen Chris shoot a man in cold blood, and, in the saloon, Chris had been ready to draw on him for no good reason. Something was wrong with his little brother and he had to find out before Chris crossed over the line for good.

There's no doubt Mort Quarry is a greedy man, Jim thought, as he rode. How far he will go to get what he wants is still a mystery. And what about Melinda? Where does she fit into this?

Jim reined up his horse under a large leafy cotton-wood tree. He propped his right leg up on the pommel of his saddle and took off his hat. Running a hand through his hair, he thought about Melinda Quarry. He tried to keep his mind on the problems at hand, but the young lady's face kept popping up in his head. She was beautiful. No, more than that, she was gorgeous, intelligent, and educated. He fought to get her out of his mind, but nothing worked.

Jim had never been in love before and he wondered how it felt. All he knew was when he thought about Melissa Quarry, he experienced a feeling that was new to him. He pulled his leg back down and took off at a trot for Panther Creek. His mind was rolling around like the cue ball on a pool table, and he felt like someone was about to strike that ball hard.

Jim counted ten adobe huts, all linked together by a wide pathway. The place looked more like a small village in Mexico than an unorganized farming community. He reckoned six of the buildings served as housing while the rest were for storage and animal shelters. He was at the edge of the village when a woman called out to him.

'*Señor, señor, buenos tardes.*' It was the woman who'd hauled the wounded man's body away. She was waving at Jim to ride to a hut she stood before. 'Hello, *señor*, come over here, please, please.'

Jim walked his horse over to the hut. 'Yes, ma'am, how is the man who was shot?'

'Come inside, *señor*, and see for yourself.'

Jim stepped out of the saddle and followed the woman into the adobe shelter. The wounded man lay on a bed in the back. He was covered from the waist down with a gray woolen blanket. A wide strip of white cloth covered his wound. Jim saw no sign of blood.

'I see the bleeding has stopped,' he said.

The woman smiled up at him, took him by the arm and led him to the man's bedside. The farmer opened his eyes as they approached.

'*Señor*, this is Manuel Cardoza,' said the lady. 'Manuel, this is the man who saved your life.'

Manuel reached up; calloused fingers took hold of Jim's hand and squeezed. His grip was weak but steady.

'My name is Jim Butler. How are you doin', *amigo*?'

'*Buen*, Señor Butler, *gracias*. I wish to thank you so much. You have saved my life. I am your servant.'

41

Jim grimaced. 'I'm glad you made it OK, *amigo*, but I don't know about this servant business. I travel alone.'

'Manuel, you must get plenty of rest. You can talk to Señor Butler sometime later. Go to sleep.' Before Manuel could protest, the woman grabbed Jim by the arm and whisked him outside.

Once they were in the open air, she introduced herself to Jim. 'Señor Butler, I am Conchita Consuelo Maria Lopez de San Martin. I am the housekeeper for Mr Armstrong at his big *rancho*. Please call me Maria.'

'Howdy, Maria. Since you have such an important job with Mr Armstrong, and you also seem to be well respected here at this village, I bet you know pretty much everything that goes on in these parts.'

'*Señor* Butler, do not waste your flowery compliments on this rose. I have more thorns than you could ever imagine.'

Jim laughed at Maria's candor.

'I apologize, ma'am. You caught me

in the watermelon patch.'

'Who are you, and why are you here, Mr Jim Butler?'

The questions caught Jim flat footed, and he jerked his head back. 'Excuse me, ma'am?'

'Was my English so poor that you did not understand what I just said, Mr Butler?'

'No ma'am, you kind of caught me off guard is all.'

'Do you have something to hide, señor?'

Jim felt like he was under investigation for a crime. 'Ma'am, Maria, I was just passin' through this country when I chanced upon them fellers hurrahing Manuel and the others. I tried to be a Good Samaritan and help out a wounded man. Why are you questioning me like I committed a crime?'

'Very well, Mr Butler, if that is your name, and I feel that it is not. I have certain powers, or visions. Intuition you might call it, but that would be incorrect. Sometimes I can see into a man's heart and even his soul. I do not know you, Mr Butler, but I know of you. I had a vision of a large man coming back into this country. He seemed a stranger to all, but he had lived here many years ago. Although he did not know it at the time, he was meant to be the savior of this land.'

'Whoa there, Maria, you're givin' me goose bumps. I think I better skedaddle out of here right now before you spook me real good. You sound like a *bruja*, a witch.'

'Señor Jim, at one time you were called Badger because you would never give up. I pray that you are the man I think you are. Mr Armstrong needs your help. His health is not good. His bones no longer support his body. The time is not so far away when he will cease to walk. Please, *por favor*, help us save the ranch.'

'Maria, I don't know what to say, except you've got me all wrong. I'm just driftin'. That's all.'

Jim quick footed it outside and swung into his saddle He tipped his hat to Maria, and dug heels into the steel dun. The big mare took off at a fast trot away from the Mexican village.

5

Early the next morning Mort Quarry rented a buckboard and drove out to the Double-A-Slash. His reason for going was to get word to his spy at the ranch, but since he had to make the trip anyway, he decided to make Bale Armstrong one final offer. If the old fool didn't accept the deal he would put himself in harm's way. It wouldn't start today, but tomorrow Mort Quarry would turn his men loose. He had over a dozen hard cases working for him; each one picked for his prowess with a six gun. All Armstrong had was a bunch of cowboys. Quarry did not expect much competition. Chris Armstrong and Dude Miller rode alongside the buckboard. Quarry didn't expect trouble, but he was prepared for anything that might happen.

'Dang your sorry hide, Valentine. You're the laziest son-of-a-gun I ever worked with. If we don't get this fence fixed today, Mr Armstrong will have our behinds.'

'Rusty Puckett, how many times I got to tell you, don't call me Valentine. Val is my name, and I ain't lazy; I just like to work real careful like so I don't have to come back and do a job twice.'

Rusty started to reply when out of the corner of his eye he caught a glimpse of movement down by a ranch gate that was a quarter mile from where they were working.

'Look yonder, Valentine. Can you make out them hombres over by the gate?'

'Why sure I can. I got eagle eyes. Let's see, that looks like,' he paused for a moment. 'One of them riders is Dude Miller, the other one is Chris.'

'Them two,' said Rusty, 'means Mort Quarry must be drivin' the rig.'

'Yep, Rusty, there ain't no mistakin' that big ol' galoot. Wonder what they're here for?'

'It sure ain't no social call. Val, I'll stay and work on this fence. You fork your bronc and beat it to the ranch house. Mr Armstrong needs to know them polecats are comin'.'

Val Rose didn't hesitate. He hit leather and was gone.

★   ★   ★

Jim Butler sat horseback high on a tree covered knoll and watched the Double-A-Slash rider take off in the direction of the ranch house. Jim rode in a zigzag pattern down through the trees, never losing sight of Val Rose or the buckboard and its two outriders. He watched as the buckboard slowed down and stopped. The driver got down and walked over behind an ancient pecan tree. In a moment, the massive man climbed back aboard the rig and resumed his journey.

Jim started to continue on when the actions of the Double-A-Slash cowhand stopped him cold. Instead of riding straight to the ranch, the man veered his horse to the tree where Mort Quarry had been just minutes ago. The puncher dismounted and went behind the huge pecan. In a moment he was back on his horse and riding again.

*   *   *

Quarry drove the buckboard up to the front door of the ranch house. He pulled a handkerchief from an inside pocket, wiped the sweat from his face, and brushed the dust off his clothes as best he could.

'Dude, go knock on the door and see if anybody's home.' Quarry laughed at his little joke. Bale Armstrong was always home. Too many hard falls from breaking wild horses had crippled him up.

Dude leaped to the ground and sauntered to the house. He banged on the heavy wooden door. 'Anybody here?' he yelled. 'Hey, open up.' He slammed his fist against the door over and over again. 'Come on and open this door before I bust it to kindling.'

Maria jerked the door open. Hate and anger smoldered in her eyes. 'You people do not belong here. You must go, now.'

'Now, now, Maria, control yourself,' said Quarry. 'If you want to keep your job when I take over this ranch, you are going to have to show my men and I a little respect.'

'I spit on your respect,' said Maria. 'Hombre, you have much money and power, but other people have power, too. You are crossing a line that should not be crossed. If you live, it will be with many regrets. You have angered the wrong people. The spirits do not lie.'

'Don't worry about her babblings, Mr Quarry,' said Chris Armstrong. 'She's about half crazy. The Mexicans think she can tell the future. I think it's a lot of bunk.'

Mort was about to tell the woman off when Bale Armstrong appeared beside her. He was carrying a double-barreled twelve gauge shotgun.

'Quarry, you and your trained monkey get off my property.' Armstrong leaned on a heavy wooden cane. His face distorted with the pain that wracked his body; his eyes shone with another kind of pain. 'Chris, son, get down and come in and let's talk.'

'I ain't got nothing to say to you that hasn't already been said.' Venom dripped from Chris Armstrong's words. 'I work for Mr Quarry now, and when he takes over the Double-A-Slash, I'll be running the outfit. Then you'll see how a ranch ought to be run.'

Dude Miller stood like a rock, staring at the twelve gauge shotgun, ready to shoot Bale Armstrong if he tried to pull the triggers. His face twitched when Chris said he would be running the Double-A-Slash, otherwise, he was a statue.

'Hold on now, Bale,' said Mort Quarry, smiling. 'There's no need to go waving a weapon around and threatening anyone. We are here to plead with you to sell us your ranch. Be reasonable, man, you are in no shape to run a property like this, and you aren't getting any younger. One of your sons is dead, and the other one has left you. Who are you saving this ranch for, the Mexican squatters over by Panther Creek?' An ugly laugh escaped through Mort Quarry's chunky lips.

'I swear on my dead son's grave,' said Bale, his face white from the pain. 'I will blow you to kingdom come if you don't ride out of here right now.' He wavered and almost fell, lowering the shotgun as he struggled for balance.

Chris Armstrong leaped from his horse and ripped the twelve gauge from his father's weakening grip. As he glowered down at this shell of a man, pity and disgust enveloped his mind, but fear showed in his eyes. Bale Armstrong had always seemed indestructible, now he seemed so small and insignificant. Chris hated him for his roughshod ways, but he loved this man as only a son could. He stood transfixed, shotgun in hand, his mind racing. Had he made the wrong decision leaving his father? He was beginning to see Mort Quarry for what he was, a ruthless, greedy monster. Was it time to go back to his father? While he stood there bewildered, Dude Miller made his move.

'Shucks, this old man ain't worth the air he's breathin',' said Dude. 'I'm gonna solve everybody's problem. I'll just kill him right here.'

Dude started toward Bale Armstrong when a screaming chunk of lead tore his hat from his head. Dude dropped to one knee and ripped his pistol from its holster. 'What in blazes is going on?' His voice was shrill, filled with fear.

Chris Armstrong pulled iron, and crouched beside his father. Maria ran to Bale and tried to shield his body with her own. Mort Quarry made no movement toward shelter. He sat immobile in the buckboard.

'Put your guns away, boys,' he said. 'Whoever is shooting at us intended that shot as a warning. Come out and show yourself, friend. I believe there is a misunderstanding here.'

Another bullet burned in inches from Mort Quarry's hand, burrowing into the side of the buckboard, slinging splinters in every direction. The horse started to buck, but Quarry got the animal under control. 'Dude, Chris,' he said, 'mount up.' He turned and looked out toward the tree lined ridge that edged across the west side above the house. 'I hope we meet again, my friend. Perhaps next time, I will have the upper hand.'

Quarry turned the buckboard around and headed away; the horse taking off at a brisk trot. Dude Miller mounted his horse, gun in hand, and rode after his boss. Chris Armstrong stood looking down at his father.

'Chris, your father, he needs you,' said Maria. 'He cannot live without you on the ranch. Please stay, Chris, *por favor.*'

Chris stared at his father with blank eyes, confusion tearing through his mind. He took a deep breath, turned, mounted his horse and rode away; he didn't look back.

6

Jim forked the steel dun and headed off in the direction of the mystery tree. Things were happening too fast. He had begun developing a plan as soon as he'd found out what was going on in the Two Bucks country. He now realized there was not enough time to implement his scheme. Drastic measures would be needed without delay. He rode along rethinking everything until he cleared a rise that was above the stand of pecan trees. Scouring the countryside and discerning no movement, Jim trotted his horse down into the *Bosque*.

★ ★ ★

Mort Quarry was furious. He swung the buggy whip and popped blisters on the back of the buckboard horse as they made their way back to Two Bucks City. His plan to take over the Double-A-Slash ranch had been fool-proof. Things had been falling into place like stacked dominoes. Now a wild card had been thrust into the mix.

Quarry had an idea that the man who'd buffaloed Dude Miller was the same one who fired from the ridge today. But who was this stranger? If it really was the gunfighter, Quick Jim Butler, where did the man come from, and what were his motives for protecting Bale Armstrong and his ranch?

Dude Miller rode in front of the buckboard; Chris Armstrong brought up the rear. Dude slowed his horse down allowing the wagon to catch up with him. He sidled his mount over close to Mort Quarry.

'What do we do now, boss?' He said.

'I'm thinking about that right now, Dude. I figured that old fool was too proud to hire protection. Looks like I underestimated him.'

Mort Quarry looked upon Bale

Armstrong in a new light. 'Let's assume Jim Butler is on the Double-A-Slash payroll.'

'Let me have him, boss.' Dude had lost a lot of respect from the Quarry men after the beating Jim gave him. 'I owe that gunslick a whippin'. He caught me off guard when I'd drunk too much of that snakehead whiskey Stretch Cassidy peddles in his saloon. I'll bust him up good, then I'll kill him.'

'Hold your horses, Dude. There'll be plenty of time for Butler. What bothers me right now is there might be more gun hands coming in to join him. It doesn't seem likely that Armstrong would hire just one man.'

'I hear tell he's a cheap ol' bird, boss. Maybe he figures one *hombre* is enough.'

Quarry ran a thick finger up and down the side of his nose. 'Yes, maybe so, but the man has enough money to hire a considerable army if he chooses to.'

Quarry didn't like being in the dark

about his opposition. He needed information from his man on the inside at the Double-A-Slash, and he needed it now. Out of sheer anger, he jerked the buckboard reins back hard, causing the horse to rear up and fight the pressure of the bit tearing at its mouth. Crazed with pain from the whipping Mort Quarry had administered, the poor animal squealed in agony, bucking and fighting to break free from the restraining harness. Quarry bounced all over the buckboard seat like a rag doll. His knuckles whitened as he held on tight to the reins to keep from getting hurled to the ground.

'Shoot the stupid beast, Dude!' Quarry yelled. 'Shoot it!'

Dude Miller peeled his six-gun from its leather pocket and blasted six chunks of lead into the crazed horse. One slug pierced the animal's brain. It dropped to the ground, quivered for a moment, and lay still.

Chris Armstrong reeled in his saddle, a look of horror masking his face. He had just witnessed the execution of an animal whose only fault was being scared and in pain.

'Filthy evil beast,' said Mort Quarry, spitting blood from where he had bitten his tongue during the commotion. He removed a handkerchief from his breast pocket and wiped the scarlet residue from his lips. Tossing the soiled cloth aside, he removed a small notebook and a pencil from an inside coat pocket and scribbled out a message.

'Dude,' he said, 'take this paper to the tree. I'll ride double with the boy and we'll meet you in town. Chris, bring your horse over here and get off. I will ride in the saddle, and you can get on behind me.'

Tight lipped and shaking, Chris rode over next to his boss and lurched to the ground. Mort Quarry swung his considerable bulk aboard Chris's mount. When Chris climbed up behind him, the horse shuddered at the extra weight. Quarry kicked the horse's ribs and the animal bolted forward toward

Two Bucks City.

When they reached the edge of town Quarry dismounted. 'Chris,' he said, 'go to the livery stable and tell Old Man Parker where he can find his buckboard. And, Chris, tell him next time I rent a rig from him, it had better have a decent horse.'

Quarry walked to his office building, which was next to the bank and checked on his messages. Upon finding none, he stepped into his private office and sat down behind his desk. He was pondering the Armstrong Ranch problem when his thoughts were interrupted by a faint knock on the door.

'Come in, Melinda,' he said, smiling.

Melinda Quarry danced through the door. 'Daddy, how did you know it was me?'

'Melinda, my dear, I can always tell by your knock, it is you. You have the soft unobtrusive ways of your mother, God rest her blessed soul. What can I do for you today, angel?'

'I brought you the documents that

you asked for on the Double-A-Slash property, and there are some loan papers that need your approval also.'

'Excellent, Melinda, you are becoming quite an astute businesswoman. Anything else new?'

'Why, yes, there is. We had a new depositor today, a new young man in town. His name is Jim Butler, and he is quite attractive in a cowboy sort of way. Although I doubt he is a cowboy. He transferred five thousand dollars from New Mexico to our bank.'

'Young, handsome, and with money. My goodness, daughter, I had better meet this fellow and see what his intentions might be. He could be after my most precious asset.'

'Oh, Daddy, you are such a silly. I just met Jim.'

'Jim, is it. Well, well, now I know I must meet Mr Butler. Is he staying in town?'

'I have no idea where Mr Butler is staying, and I don't care.' Melinda said, looking flustered by her father's response. 'I have too much work on my desk to be gossiping with you, Father. If you need me, call.' With that, the young lady made a rapid exit.

Mort Quarry rubbed his chin as his daughter stomped out of the room. 'Yes,' he said, 'I will check out Mr Jim Butler.'

* * *

Late in the afternoon, Jim rode into Two Bucks City. He was dusty and near worn out. After settling his horse into the livery stable, he walked to the Quarry hotel and got a second story room. He ordered a bathtub and lots of hot water to be sent up to the room. Waiting for the tub, he lay down and took a short nap.

* * *

Darkness lay like a shroud over Two Bucks City; dense cobalt blue clouds rolled in promising much needed rain.

Jim Butler, all clean and spiffy after his bath, stepped out of the Calico Kitchen restaurant and breathed in the cool damp air. Inhaling brought about a chill that started in his lungs and ricocheted throughout his whole body. He shivered. The shiver was not entirely caused by the liquid night air. Jim's father was in a tight situation, and it was going to take all of Jim's cunning and resourcefulness to pull him out. Chris was setting himself up for trouble, also.

Jim's steps were heavy as he plodded along the creaking plank sidewalk toward the Golden Ace. When he reached the saloon, he recognized two of the horses that were tied to a hitching rail out front. Peering over the swinging doors, he saw the owners of the horses standing at the bar. He swore under his breath, hitched up his gun belt, and stepped inside.

7

The saloon was brimming with patrons. Jim recognized some of the men from his previous encounter with Dude Miller. Over in a far corner, he noticed his old friend Shank Halsey playing cards with three other men. One of the other card players was Rusty Puckett. The third man was the one who had retrieved the note Mort Quarry had left in the mystery tree. The fourth player was unknown to Jim. Down at the far end of the bar were two rough looking hombres. They were the ones whose horses Jim had recognized. The two men were drinking beer and talking loud. Jim sidled up to the end of the bar that was closest to the swinging doors.

'Howdy there, feller,' said Stretch. 'How 'bout a beer on me? It's still the coldest in town.'

'I thank you, sir,' said Jim, 'but

there's no need to give away your profit. I can pay.' Jim plunked a handful of coins onto the bar.

'Next round, my friend. This one's on me. I never thought I would see the day when Dude Miller got his comeuppance. A word to the wise, though. There's Armstrong men in here tonight, and Quarry men, too. They don't get along none too well. Chris Armstrong's over in the corner gettin' pie-eyed drunk. It could get real ugly in here tonight. I'm keeping my Greener right close at hand, just in case. Better not drink too much so's you lose your edge. It just might be fatal.'

'Thanks for the warning,' Jim answered.

Stretch Cassidy nodded and moved away. Jim began to drink the beer, lost in his thoughts.

Out of nowhere, the face of Melinda Quarry sprang into Jim's consciousness. He gave himself a mental slap to drive her from his thoughts and chugged the remaining contents of the mug. He was about to order another one when

Stretch appeared, fresh mug in hand. Jim insisted upon paying for this second mug and after mild protest, the bartender accepted the payment.

The lanky bartender leaned down until his long hound dog face was inches from Jim's. 'You see those two gunnies at the other end of the bar? They're a couple of real bad ones. The big one is Hack Bonner. Man, he must weigh near two hundred and fifty pounds. They say it's all muscle and he knows how to use it. Cat quick with a short gun too. Fast as he is, he ain't near as swift as that skinny one standin' beside him. That one's name is McCafferty, but he goes by the handle of The Irish Kid. Some say he's the fastest man with a short gun anywhere. They rode in this afternoon. Rumor has it they are here to run Bale Armstrong out of the country. If that's true, there's gonna be a whole bunch of innocent people in a lot of trouble. Bale Armstrong is the last chance this town has to keep Mort Quarry from owning everything. He wants my saloon but I ain't sellin' unless Armstrong gets whipped. If he loses his ranch, well . . . ' Stretch Cassidy's voice trailed off into silence. Fear showed in his eyes. He lowered his head and walked away.

A loud commotion from the opposite end of the bar grabbed everybody's attention, including Jim's. The big gunslinger and the little one were arguing.

'I know you're fast, Kid, but there are those that's faster.' The sound rumbled like thunder rolling from the mouth of the big man, Hack Bonner.

'Ain't nobody faster than the Irish Kid,' said the skinny one in a thick Irish brogue. He was shuffling his feet and wiggling his long bony fingers.

'There's one for sure who is,' Hack Bonner said.

'I said there ain't a livin' soul who can pull iron with me.'

'I heard you crawfished to Jim Butler over Arizona way a year or two back.'

Cormac McCafferty, alias the Irish

Kid, turned purple. 'That's a bald faced lie. I never even seen Jim Butler. And if I ever did come up against that faker, I'd back him down so quick it would make his dear sainted mother's head swim. That's a fact, boyo.'

Chris Armstrong was headed up to the bar for another bottle of red eye when he overheard the gunmen's conversation. He had seen Jim Butler come into the saloon, but hadn't had the nerve to approach him.

'Say there, fellers,' he said, his speech slurring. 'I heard you boys talkin' about the great Jim Butler, and how fast he was with a six-gun.'

'You got a problem with that, son?' Hack Bonner towered over Chris's six feet like some malevolent giant.

'No, sir, I sure don't. It's just that I thought you'd like to know that ol' Jim Butler, himself, is right here in this saloon this very night.' Chris beamed like he'd just swallowed the prize canary.

'Where's he at?' It was the Irish Kid.

He was all business.

Chris pointed a wobbly finger at Jim. The bar top cleared in an instant with everybody moving into the crowd around the poker tables. Shank Halsey grabbed Rusty Puckett by the shirtsleeve and yanked him out of his chair. Playing cards flew in every direction. Puckett started to protest when Shank whispered something into his ear. Rusty Puckett gasped and stared at Jim Butler. His eyes slowly filled with recognition, and a smile cracked the corners of his mouth. The two old cowboys edged up closer to the front of the crowd.

Jim stood rooted in place. The saloon got coffin quiet, as the Irish Kid swaggered towards Jim. Stretch Cassidy let his hands rest on the Greener shotgun under the bar.

'You Jim Butler?' asked the Kid.

No answer.

'Look at him, Irish,' said Bonner. 'He's too danged scared to talk.'

'You a coward, Butler?' It was the Kid again. 'You don't look like no big time killer to me. I think your reputation must have been made on farmers and store keepers. That sound about right. Yeah, I think that's right. What do you think, Hack?'

'He don't look like no bad man I ever seen, Kid. He looks, to me, like he wants to leave this fine gathering.'

Jim Butler still did not move or speak.

'All right, boys, the party's over. No one gets killed in my place if I can help it.' Stretch pointed his Greener right at the Irish Kid's belt line. 'Butler, you best back out of here and ride while you still can. I'll hold off these boys. Go, now.'

Jim hesitated a moment then began to slide backwards out thru the swinging doors. Once outside, he disappeared into the night.

'I'll be hogtied if I ain't ever seen a man run so fast in my life,' said Hack Bonner. 'It was sure a sight to see.' He was laughing and slapping the Irish Kid on the back. 'Come on, Irish, I'm gonna buy you the biggest piece of cow they got in this town.'

Both men headed out of the Golden Ace, spurs jangling and jaws flapping, headed for the closest open café.

'Did you see it, boys? Did you see it?' Chris Armstrong was roaring drunk and spouting off. 'Mr High and Mighty Jim Butler has a yellow streak when he has to face a real man. I should have gunned him down the other day when I had a chance. Next time I see him I might just make him eat dirt. That sure would be a funny sight, wouldn't it boys?'

Shank Halsey and Rusty Puckett stomped out of the saloon. They had just seen their old friend 'Badger' Armstrong crawfish, and their night of fun was over.

Chris whispered something to the men closest to him and they erupted with laughter. He raised his hands for them to be quiet and then he weaved his way up to the bar. 'Say, there, Cassidy,' said Chris, trying to look serious, but not succeeding. 'How come it is that you always pull out that old shotgun every time somebody sneezes in your saloon? We all know you ain't got the guts to use it.'

'One of you men take this boy home before he makes a statement he can't back up,' said Stretch.

A couple of the more sober looking Quarry men got up and started towards Chris. One was Charley Pratt.

Chris was not ready to go. 'I ain't leaving here 'till I'm blamed good and ready.' He pulled iron and waved it at the two approaching Quarry men.

'Come on now, Chris,' said Charley Pratt. 'Mr Quarry will skin you alive if he finds out you been raisin' a ruckus in the saloon. Come on, go with us. I got a bottle in my room. We can keep on drinkin' there.'

'Mr Quarry,' said Chris, in mocking tones. 'He ain't nothing but a horse shooter. Yeah, a horse killer, that's all your Mr Quarry is. Well, my name ain't Quarry. It's Armstrong, Chris Armstrong,

73

and me and my daddy got the best ranch in the whole panhandle country. You can tell Mr Horse Murderer that I'm going back where I belong, the Double-A-Slash ranch. And Charley Pratt, you little weasel, you tell ol' horse killer that he ain't welcome on that ranch anymore. If I see him I'll shoot him on sight.'

Chris was still waving his pistol around and staggering all about. Stretch rolled his Greener over the bar top and pointed it at the drunken man. Chris caught the movement out of the corner of his eye and snapped a shot in that direction. The slug hit Cassidy high in the chest. He reeled against the back bar and dropped to the floor. His bartender rushed over and kneeled beside him.

'Somebody get Doc Whithers, quick! I think Stretch is dying.'

'Oh, my Lord,' yelled Charley Pratt. 'Some of you boys grab the kid and get him out of town.'

'Where do we take him?'

'Take him to that line shack up in the hills. I'll get Mr Quarry.'

A dozen hands latched on to Chris Armstrong, who, in his drunken state, continued to protest. They hoisted him up on their shoulders and carried him out to the horses. In a flash they were gone.

Charley Pratt looked dazed as he stumbled out into the crisp night air. He mounted his horse and took off at a gallop to find his boss.

8

Bam! Bam! Bam! The banging noise woke Mort Quarry up. He had snoozed off while reading the paper. 'Just a minute, I'm coming. Hold your horses.' He did not like to be disturbed at home. The squalid face of Charley Pratt met his gaze as he peered through the peep hole. Quarry wrenched the door open.

'Charley Pratt, this had better be important.'

'Y-yes sir, Mr Quarry, it is real important. Chris Armstrong done got himself all likkered up and shot Stretch Cassidy down at his bar.'

'What! How in the devil's name did that happen?'

Charley Pratt relayed the story while Mort Quarry listened in stoic silence. When Pratt finished, Quarry rubbed his chin and pursed his lips.

'Charley, you did the right thing getting that idiot out to the line shack. I want you to ride out there and assign two of the men to stay with Chris. They had better not let him out of their sight. If they do it will be on your head.'

'Yes, sir, I'll take care of it. What if Cassidy kicks off, boss? What'll we do then?'

'Leave that problem up to me. Now, you had better get out of here right away.'

Charley started to go when Quarry grabbed his arm in a vice-like grip. Charley almost cried out in pain. Mort Quarry got right up in the small man's face.

'Charley, do you know where Dude is?'

'Yes, sir, I do.'

'Before you leave for the shack, get one of the boys to round him up. Tell him to meet me in the Golden Ace. Understand?'

Charley nodded yes, and Quarry turned him loose.

Hack Bonner and the Irish Kid walked out of the Calico Kitchen café rubbing their full stomachs and moaning about how much they had eaten.

'Dang, ol' son,' said Bonner, 'skinny as you are, I don't know where you put all them vittles. You got a hollow leg, Kid?'

'You know I don't eat real often, Hack, but when I do, I don't mess around.'

Both gunmen laughed and started in the direction of the saloon. They ambled along the dark wooden sidewalk talking and taking in the cool night air.

'Say, Kid, you ever seen anything as funny as Jim Butler tonight. I couldn't hardly keep from laughin' out loud.'

'Yeah, me too. I believe that was the best job of crawfishin' I ever saw. He didn't say a word, just pulled in his feelers and slid out backwards. I thought I was gonna bust a gut.'

'You boys think that was real funny, don't you?'

The voice came from the shadows of an alley on their right. The click of a revolver being cocked echoed off the dry boards of the buildings siding the alley. The two men froze in place.

'You two funny boys turn around and back over here into this alley. We got to have us a little palaver. I see your right hand twitchin', Cormac. A wise man never shoots at what he can't see. Be easy.'

Careful to not make any false moves, the men eased their way backwards into the alley. They were ten paces in when the voice told them to stop and turn around.

'Howdy, fellers, how are y'all doin'?' It was Jim Butler.

'I knew it was you,' said the Irish Kid. 'You are the only person in the world, besides my sainted mother, who calls me by my real name.'

'Dang, Jim, you sure had us buffaloed.'

Hack Bonner had his hat off and was scratching his balding head. 'Son, I'm gettin' way too old for these kinds of shenanigans.'

'Sorry, Hack, but it just had to look real tonight. Hopefully, the Quarry bunch will be so confused about me that they'll lay off, and I can have time to find out where my dad and my brother stand in all this. Y'all got here quicker than I thought you would. Bartender said you rode in this afternoon.'

'We been in that bar raisin' Old Ned since around three o'clock. We were gettin' hungry and thinkin' maybe you weren't comin'. We were about to head out for some grub when you showed up. What's so important that you had to call me and the Kid in on it?'

'It's a long story, Hack. So I'll just hit the high points.'

Jim told his friends the story in as few words as possible.

'So that's why I don't want anyone to know who I am, just yet,' he said, as he finished.

The Irish Kid whistled through his

teeth. 'You sure have you a mountain-sized problem there, Jim boy. That's for sure.'

'Kid,' said Hack Bonner, scowling at the Kid's last statement, 'you've always had a way of statin' the obvious. Yeah, Jim's got a problem, and if he's got a problem, well then, we got a problem too.'

'I know that,' the Kid said, looking like he had just been scolded by his mama.

'You two cut it out,' said Jim. 'I knew you would help me so I worked out a plan for when y'all showed up. Our little ruckus in the saloon tonight was the beginning of that plan.'

He was about to explain his idea when they heard someone out on the street. The three men backed against a building and held their breaths. Two men walked by chattering like bluejays at a church picnic.

'I was there, I tell you.' It was a short dumpy hostler from the livery. 'I saw it all. That Armstrong kid shot Stretch

Cassidy in cold blood. Ol' Stretch never had a chance.'

'Is he dead?' said the other man. Jim did not recognize him.

'Lord knows. They carried him over to Doc Wither's place. I reckon he's still there. That is unless the undertaker already has him.'

'Stretch was a good man. They catch that kid, they'll hang him for sure.'

The men disappeared down the street. Jim took off his hat and ran a hand through his hair. 'Stretch dead and Chris on the run for his murder. Something isn't right. Did you boys see any of this?'

'No, Jimmy, we left right after you did.'

'Your brother was sure snookered when we left the saloon. He was rantin' on about you bein' a coward and all. Said he knew that you wasn't no man. He said . . . '

'All right, Cormac, I get the idea,' said Jim. 'Be quiet while I think this out.'

The Irish Kid started to say something else when Hack Bonner grabbed his shoulder and squeezed. Jim stood in silence for a long time before he spoke.

'Hack, I want you to ride out to the Double-A-Slash ranch and tell my father you are an old saddle pal of mine looking for work. If he hasn't heard about Chris, tell him. There is an old friend of mine cowboyin' there named Shank Halsey. He knows I'm alive. Get with him and anybody he can trust and y'all wait for word from me.'

'Cormac, I want you to hire on with Mort Quarry's bunch. Tell him you and Hack split up. You'll think of a reason why. Try and find out where they are hiding Chris. I'm going to the doctor's and check on Stretch. I'll be in touch.'

Double-checking that the street was deserted, Hack and Cormac drifted out in five minute intervals. Jim edged down to the back of the alley and scooted along the shadows behind the buildings until he came to Doc Wither's place.

Jim crept up the side of the building and peered around the front. The street was empty. He could see lights coming from the saloon, and from the sound roaring out of the place, everything was going strong despite the earlier shooting. Stepping up onto the sidewalk he peeped through a window. Lights were on in the back room. Jim knocked on the doctor's front door. In a moment a shuffling noise brought someone to the door.

'What now?' said an old man in a night shirt, as he opened the door.

'I came to check on Mr Cassidy,' said Jim.

The doctor looked this stranger up and down. He moved the lamp he was carrying close to Jim's face. Jim raised his hand to shield the light from his eyes.

'Good Lord, Almighty!' said Doc Withers. 'You're Badger Armstrong.'

9

'Come on in here, son. Stretch is in the back room. He's lost a lot of blood, but the bullet didn't hit any vital organs. He ought to be OK with some rest.'

'Doc, they say Chris shot him in cold blood. Is that true?'

'That's what I was told, Badger, but I don't know for sure.' Doc Withers pointed to a chair. 'Set down son, I was just about to have a cup of coffee. I'll fix you one, too.'

The doctor poured two cups of the steaming black liquid and handed one to Jim. He stepped around behind a worn maple desk and sat down with a groan.

'Bale Armstrong Jr.,' he said, 'what in the world are you doing here? I see the rumors of your demise were premature, so I won't even get into that. You look different than the last time I saw you.

What was it, twelve, fifteen years ago?'

Doc Withers took another sip of his coffee, and Jim got a chance to talk. 'How did you recognize me, Doc?'

'When I flashed the lamplight on to your face I knew you looked familiar, a face from out of the past. I raised the light up to get a closer look and you shaded your face with your left hand. I recognized the barb wire scars across your palm; that's when it came to me. You were ten years old when that old mossy horn steer knocked your horse down and butted you into that barb wire fence around that pond up by Panther creek. You remember that? Boy, you were cut up all over the place. Thank God the only bad cuts were on your hand. It took a right smart of stitches to close that up if I recollect right.'

'Yes, sir, it did. Are you sure Stretch is gonna be OK?'

'He's got the best doctor in these parts. 'Course, he's got the only doctor in these parts.' Doc Withers chuckled at his attempt at humor.

Jim felt he could trust the old doctor; he really didn't have much choice since he had been recognized. He told Doc Withers what was happening to his father and how Mort Quarry was tied into it. Doc sat silent, cradling his cup and listening. When Jim finished, the sawbones got up and poured himself another shot of coffee. Jim declined.

'Badger,' said Doc, his face grim, 'I've been watching this problem develop for some time now. Your father is a tough man, but he's also an old man. He fought his wars forty years ago, and he shouldn't have to fight again.

'When the railroad bypassed us for Amarillo, the future of this county looked grim. Mort Quarry came to Two Bucks City, and we all hailed him as a savior of the town. He brought money, established a bank, as well as other businesses, and had some innovative ideas on how to put the town back on the map. He loaned ranchers money, renovated the local church out of his own pocket, brought in his daughter to teach school, and, most important, he gave the community hope.'

'What changed everything?'

'Mort Quarry bought a couple hundred acres of land. He even paid cash. Said he wanted to start a small herd and hired a bunch of men to work the place. After a while, ranchers started losing cattle; a few at first, then whole herds began to disappear into the night. Supposedly, Quarry even lost part of his herd. Before anybody realized what was happening, all of the ranchers in these parts that had notes at the bank, got behind. Turns out the fine print in the loan contracts stated that if the note payment became three days late, the bank could foreclose. And that's just what happened.'

This time Jim said yes to another cup of coffee. Stretch groaned in the back room and Doc Withers walked back to take a look. Jim mulled over what he had just been told. After a moment,

Doc called him from the back room. Cassidy was awake.

'He heard your voice and wanted to talk to you, son. He's weak from the blood loss, so you can only talk a couple of minutes.'

'Thanks, Doc.' Jim knelt down by the bed and stared at the wounded man. He thought Stretch was asleep. Jim started to rise when the saloon owner spoke. His voice was shallow but clear.

'Jim, Jim, I've got to know. When you backed down from those two gunnies, were you scared or was it another reason? I can't believe you're yellow, Jim.' Stretch struggled to finish what he had to say. 'You've got something else in mind. Am I right?'

Jim wasn't sure what to say. He nodded his head. Stretch reached up and with a feeble grasp closed his massive hand around Jim's. Bony fingers dug into Jim's wrist then the hand went limp and fell back to the bed. Jim looked up at the doctor, his eyes wide with apprehension.

'No, he's not dead, Badger, he just needs a lot of rest.' Doc Withers sipped his ever present cup of coffee. 'You better get out of here, Badger, before someone else decides to check on Cassidy. Don't worry, he'll be safe here. I'm the only doctor for a hundred miles, and Mort Quarry knows it. He won't mess with me.'

'Thanks, Doc, I appreciate your help. I will be going now.'

'Badger, one more thing, have you talked to your father? Because you two were estranged when we thought you had been killed, he took your death real hard. Never was the same after that. Now with Chris messed up, I don't know what will happen to him. Go to your dad, son. If not for you, then do it for him. He deserves to know you're alive.'

Jim nodded and stepped out into the darkness. He was about to round the corner of the building when a voice stopped him in his tracks. He turned to see Melinda Quarry approaching from across the street.

'Mr Butler, Jim, hello. Remember me, Melinda from the bank?'

'Yes, ma'am, I remember you, Miss Quarry.' Jim had drunk three cups of coffee, and, yet, his mouth was as dry as the Sonora desert.

'I saw the doctor's light on and thought I would check on poor Mr Cassidy. How is he, Jim?'

Jim Butler shuddered every time Melinda Quarry spoke his name. He was experiencing a strange feeling that he had not felt before. Jim fought back the urge to stutter as his brain had difficulty forming words.

'Doc says he will live. He's a lucky man. If he hadn't have been so tall, the bullet would've hit him in the head.'

'Oh, I am so glad to hear that. Mr Cassidy seems like such a good man. It is so unfortunate that he was shot in his own place of business.'

'Yes, ma'am,' Jim struggled for words. He needed to get out of town to clear his head. 'That was a terrible accident — Stretch getting shot like that. Liquor can do outlandish things to a man.'

'My father said it wasn't an accident.'

'What do you mean, Miss Quarry?'

'Call me Melinda, and I will tell you, Jim.'

Jim took a deep breath and let it out slow. 'Melinda,' he said, trying to smile.

'My father says Chris Armstrong shot Mr Cassidy because his father and Mr Cassidy were having a feud. First thing in the morning the sheriff is going to put a posse together and search for Chris. When they find him they will hang him.'

'Hang him without a trial? They can't do that.'

'My father says it will send a message to Mr Bale Armstrong and the other bad men in this county that we are tired of all the rustling and killing. In order to maintain law and order, sometimes you have to take the law into your own hands.'

'That's what your father says, huh?

You agree with him, Melinda?'

'My father is never wrong, Jim. But enough of this morbid talk. I am pleased that Mr Cassidy is going to recover. Let's celebrate. The café is still open. I will let you buy me a cup of coffee and a piece of their wonderful pie.' Melinda held out her hand.

'No, ma'am.' The words surprised Jim as they came out. 'I have something important to do. I will see you tomorrow, maybe.' He reached out and shook Melinda's hand, and he was gone.

Jim trotted back to his horse, mounted and rode out of town. He let the mare have her head to run, while his mind raced through the recent happenings. This night had succeeded only in muddying up the water. Jim did not believe the story about the feud between his father and the saloon keeper. Chris was a hot-headed kid, but he wasn't a murderer. Melinda Quarry believed her father was perfect. How could a beautiful intelligent girl be so naïve? And those weird feelings, was he in love with her? He fought to clear his head as he rode toward the Double-A-Slash.

10

Brilliant sunlight decorated the hillside as it filtered down in curious patterns through the broad black-jack leaves. The grass stood tall after a shower of morning dew. Jim Butler shivered from the early chill and rolled over in his blankets. As a rule, he was up well before dawn and off about his business. This night he had slept little, his mind churning thoughts concerning the coming day. He was anxious about the forthcoming meeting with his father. Fifteen years had been a long time. He had left as a headstrong boy. He returned as a man who had experienced both the good and the bad side of life. Now, he felt like he was somewhere in the middle with no direction to go.

Jim made a small quick fire and boiled coffee. While the bitter black grounds rolled in the bubbling hot water, he tended to his horse's needs and struck camp. The coffee ready, Jim drank two steaming cups so fast he burned his mouth. Throwing out the remainder of his breakfast, Jim smothered the fire and secured his coffee pot and tin cup in his saddlebags. He threw a leg over the steel dun mare and turned her in the direction of the Double-A-Slash ranch house.

The half-mile ride down a gentle slope took Jim past the edge of a corral. Three men were working there. Two replaced worn boards where the horses had eaten through them, while the third was whitewashing the new boards.

'Gosh durn it, Rusty, if you can't hold these boards straight, I'll get the new feller to help me, and you can do the paintin'.'

'Well, Shank Halsey, my old granny is ninety-seven years old and she could hammer a nail better than you.'

The third man, new hire, Hack Bonner looked at the men and shook his head. 'Say, boys,' he said, 'we got company.'

'You two ain't changed one bit when it comes to gettin' along. Folks that don't know y'all would think you two ol' boys don't much like each other.' Jim grinned down at his old friends. 'Rusty Puckett, how in the world are you doin'?'

'My goodness gracious, son, look at you,' said Rusty. 'You done all growed up. I'm fine, Badger, now that you're here. I was in the saloon the other night when that ruckus broke out between you and Hack over there and your other *compadre*. You sure had us fooled, Badger.'

Shank Halsey broke into the conversation. 'Hack told us all about your plan, Badger. Me and Rusty are with you all the way. Most of the other hands will be too when they find out you're throwin' in with the Double-A-Slash. When are we gonna go and run that Quarry bunch out of the county for good?'

'Hold up there, Shank. We don't have any concrete proof that Quarry is running a crooked outfit. We've got to catch him or his men in action.'

'Me and Rusty would've done called Quarry's hand, but Bale works us so dang hard, when we ain't workin', we're restin'.'

'Boys, I'd like to jaw with you, but I have a chore I've got to get done.'

'You goin' to see your daddy?' asked Hack.

'Yep, I am.'

'He wasn't goin' to hire me, but the señora that takes care of him talked him into it. She said she had a vision about savin' the ranch and I was a part of it. I ain't afraid of no man, but she made my skin crawl. You be careful, Jim.'

Jim nodded to his friends and rode up to the ranch house. He dismounted, tied his horse and walked up to an ornate wooden door. Taking a deep breath, he knocked three times. In a moment, the massive door swung open. Maria stood in the doorway.

'*Buenos dias*, Señor Butler,' she said, 'please, come in. *Mi casa es su casa.*'

'Thank you, Maria. I need to speak with my fath . . . uh, Mr Armstrong, please.'

'Most certainly, *señor*, come and sit in the parlor. Mr Armstrong is in the kitchen. I will get him. And, please, be gentle with him; he is not well. *Comprende, jefe?*'

Jim flinched, almost dropping the hat he held in his hands. 'I understand Maria, but why did you call me boss?'

'Are you not Bale Armstrong Jr.?' Maria smiled revealing perfect ivory white teeth. Then she was gone.

Jim stood stunned. How did this woman know his true identity? Was she a real *bruja*, a Spanish witch? He pondered what he was going to say to his father when the thump-thumping of a wooden cane announced Bale Armstrong's arrival.

The owner of the Double-A-Slash had once been a powerful man, both physically and politically. At one time he had controlled most of the land in Deaf Smith County and all of the politicians. Bale Armstrong had lived past his time. People had died; times had changed. Now he faced an uncertain future.

'I hired a man yesterday, and I don't need any more hands,' he said, his voice still oak strong. 'I reckon you made the ride out to my ranch for the exercise, son. I thank you for coming, good bye.' The old man started to turn toward the kitchen.

'I'm not here for a job,' Jim fought to control his intense emotion. 'Papa, it's me — Badger. I've come home.'

Bale Armstrong's face turned to stone. He stared at Jim, eyes filled with hate and just a little sadness.

'Maria!' he hollered. 'Get Shank and that new man, Bonner, in here right now.'

He hobbled closer to Jim, holding his cane like a club. 'Mister, my son, Bale Armstrong Jr., has been dead and buried for a long time. He was killed in

Arizona; I saw his grave. I don't know if Mort Quarry sent you, or what, and I don't care. But if you don't get off of my property this minute, I swear to you, you will be buried here.'

Bale Armstrong made a move like he was falling. Jim reached out to catch his father, but the old fox was faking. As soon as Jim's hands were in the air, Bale hit him across the face with his cane. Jim staggered backwards, tried to maintain his balance, and dropped to one knee. He looked up just in time to see the cane flailing at his head again. Blackness enveloped him and he was out.

★   ★   ★

Dude Miller made his way through the briars and the creosote bushes up to the old line shack. He rode to within ten yards of the rickety tar paper hovel when a hail from the inside brought him to a halt.

'Who's out there?' The caller's voice

was shrill and high pitched.

'It's me, Dude. Charley Pratt you idjit, I'm comin' in.'

'OK, OK, Dude, come on.' Charley turned to the other two men there. 'It's OK, boys. It's my pardner, Dude Miller.'

Dude stepped down from his saddle, loose wrapped his horse's reins and stomped inside the small one room building. The place reeked of human filth and tobacco. Three bedrolls lay about in a haphazard manner. An old rickity table was pushed against one front corner. Two men sat on empty whiskey crates at the table. Chris Armstrong lay bound on the floor by the back wall. Charley Pratt stood in the middle of the room.

'What in the devil is that boy doin' tied up?' Dude had to do a little play acting.

'But, Dude,' said Charley, 'I thought Mr Quarry wanted him tied 'til we decided what we was gonna do with him.'

'Charley Pratt, you can't do anything right. You are the biggest foul up I know. You other two boys are relieved. Go into town, have a couple of drinks on the boss, then get some rest. We got somethin' big comin' up, real soon.'

The two waddies grabbed up their stuff and high-tailed it out of the shack. Charley Pratt hung his head and hurried over to untie Chris Armstrong.

Chris sat up and rubbed his wrists and ankles. He tried to stand, got his legs tangled up and fell. On his hands and knees, Chris wretched his guts out.

Dude watched the boy puke and laughed. 'Charley, pick up our hung-over friend here, and help him to the table. Then you clean up the mess he just made.'

With Charley's help, Chris managed to stagger to a whiskey crate and sit down.

'What's goin' on, Dude?' Chris's voice squeaked when he talked. 'Why was I all trussed up like that?

Somebody better be quick with some explaining.'

'Charley made a mistake, Chris. Mr Quarry told him to bring you up to this old line shack and keep you hid out until we see if Cassidy kicks the bucket or not. Heck, ol' Charley ain't all there sometimes. He just made the wrong decision, that's all.'

'I'm plumb sorry, Chris,' said Charley, sticking out his hand.

Chris glared at the little man but made no move to shake his hand. Charley shrugged and dropped it to his side. Dude patted Chris on the back while motioning with his head for Charley to go outside. Once the little gunman had gone, Dude sat down opposite Chris.

'Chris, the boss thinks a lot of you. We got a big deal comin' up and he wants you to ramrod the whole shootin' match.'

'Why me?' Chris said. 'What have I done to make him think I can run anything?'

'Aw, Chris, you know he's always liked you. He knows your old man never gave you a fair shake. How would you like to be runnin' the Double-A-Slash?'

'I will be someday.' The bile-coated words escaped from the bitter young man's mouth like evil spirits. 'My father's too old and feeble to run the ranch much longer. Soon it will be mine. Then, maybe I'll partner up with Mr Quarry, and we can share the biggest spread in the panhandle.'

'Yeah, yeah, now you're thinkin', Chris. That's just what Mr Quarry wants, except he's not a patient man. He doesn't want you havin' to wait a year, maybe longer, for your ranch. He wants you to have it now. That's why he wants you to lead our next job. It'll be the biggest one yet.'

Dude had the boy right where he wanted him and he knew it. The kid's greed would be his own downfall. 'Charley,' Dude hollered, 'quit your easdroppin' and come in here and fix us a pot of coffee. Me and your new boss got a heap of talkin' to do.'

Charley Pratt shuffled into the shack and started a pot of coffee, just like he was told to do.

11

Jim groaned, as he struggled back from the shadowy emptiness. He jerked his eyes open and, just as quick, closed them again. Light pierced his corneas like white hot needles. For an instant, Jim thought he was blind. He raised his eyelids, slower this time. The brightness hurt, but his vision was creeping back. First he saw shadows, and then everything began to take shape. Maria was sitting beside him with a glass in her hand.

'Welcome back, *señor*, I have some water here. You must drink. Just a little bit, *por favor*.' She held the glass up to Jim's lips and he swallowed some of the water. 'There, that is enough for now. I will give you more in a moment.'

Maria sat the water down and adjusted a damp cloth on Jim's forehead. Her eyes transfixed upon

Jim's head in an unworldly gaze, and her knobby hands moved over his aching skull, working to ease his pain.

Jim shut his eyes and kept them closed until a familiar voice caused him to rouse.

'For a little while, Badger, we thought the old rascal had punched your ticket.' Shank leaned over and touched Jim's shoulder. 'Whatever you said to him sure turned his mean light on. If me and the boys hadn't come in here quick when he hollered for us, he might have finished what he started. What got him goin', Badger?'

Jim's mouth was still full of cotton. He drank another sip of water and coughed. Even swallowing hurt. His head weighed two hundred pounds, but he managed to turn it far enough to see Shank, Rusty and Hack standing beside him.

'I told him who I was.' The words came out soft and sounded strange to Jim, like he was talking using someone else's voice. 'He told me to get out, and he started to fall. I reached out to help him and the rest is just a blur. Did he hit me?'

Shank told him what had taken place in as few words as possible. Jim was still a little groggy, but he understood what had happened. He stared up at Maria after Shank finished. He wanted to thank her for her kindness, but his voice was gone.

'You will be well soon, *señor*. Mr Armstrong is angry and confused. He thinks his mind is playing tricks on him. He will accept you, but it will take time. He carries much fear and bitterness in his heart.' Maria reached down and caressed Jim's cheek. 'Do you not feel much better than you did moments ago, *señor*?'

'Yes, yes I do. What did you do that took away the pain, Maria?'

'I did little, *señor*, perhaps your injuries were not as serious as first thought. I do not know. I am only an aged housekeeper, nothing more.'

With Shank's help, Jim rolled over

and sat up on the edge of the sofa. He stood up and found his legs shaky, but serviceable.

'Thanks for your help, Maria. I reckon I'd better be goin' before my father finds out I'm awake. I don't need another conk on the noggin today.'

Maria nodded, and Jim and the other men walked through the hallway and out of the house. They were barely outside when a rider came in from the east. Jim mounted his horse as the rider pulled to a halt next to him.

'Hey, what's goin' on here?' said Valentine Rose. 'That new waddy was supposed to relieve me up in the breaks an hour ago. I ain't had my breakfast, yet.'

He glared over at Hack Bonner. Hack threw a look at Val Rose that could have withered a prickly pear. The puncher's eyes went to the ground like a whipped pup. The corners of Hack Bonner's mouth crinkled up in a grin. He looked over at Shank.

'Go on out there, Hack,' said Shank.

'We wouldn't want Valentine to starve.'

'Valentine,' said Hack Bonner, looking perplexed, 'ain't that a girl's name?' He stared back up at the new rider, an odd look on his face.

Val Rose snorted and dug heels in his horse's flanks. It just so happened, his mount had a sore rib from getting kicked inside the corral the night before. Val hit the horse right on top of that bruised rib and that hay burner broke loose bucking like his tail was on fire, jumping and hopping all over the place. Val was a fair to middlin' rider, but he wasn't any kind of bronc peeler. He made the first two jumps, but on the third one he blew both stirrups, and on the fourth, when the horse came down, Val stayed up in the air. When he hit the ground, he bounced and smacked down on his face. He didn't move.

Hack trotted over to check on him. He reported back that Valentine didn't look too good, but he was still pumpin' air. Shank shook his head and sighed.

'I don't like that man.' Shank said. 'There's somethin' about the chowder head that don't smell right, and I ain't talkin' about his bathin' habits, neither.'

'Shank,' said Jim, 'I think that man works for Mort Quarry.' He told Shank and the others what he had seen take place at the message tree.

'I'll be dipped,' said Shank. 'I know just which pecan tree you're talkin about, too. We been gettin' good papershells off that tree for twenty years. It's down in a little sink hole with half a dozen other old pecan trees.'

'Let's go tear down his meat house,' said Rusty. 'I get first turn.'

'Wait a minute, boys. Let's think about this situation,' said Jim. 'We know who he is workin' for, but we don't know his real purpose here. Rusty, I think you need to keep an eye on our friend Valentine and see what he is up to.'

'I'll start right now.' Rusty Puckett wallowed his hat down over his ears like he was getting ready to bust a bad bronco, and stomped off towards the cook shack.

Watching him go, Shank said, 'Who's gonna watch that wall-eyed cuss.'

Jim, still astride his mount, nodded goodbye and rode off towards Two Bucks City. He was more confused about what to do now than he was before his abortive meeting with his father. Jim hadn't expected to be embraced with open arms, but he sure hadn't planned for the caning he had received at his dad's hands. He was hurting, inside and out. As he rode up into the trees, he wondered where they had stashed his brother. He hoped Cormac had been able to join the gang. Maybe he would have some answers.

★　★　★

'Yes, sir, Mr Quarry, that Armstrong boy fell for the whole thing. He thinks I came into town to get the final orders from you.'

113

'Outstanding, Dude, this calls for a drink.'

Mort Quarry reached into a burled oak liquor cabinet and drew out a bottle of ancient Scotch whiskey. He put two short glasses on the table; half filling one glass, he handed it to his *segundo*. Leaving the other glass empty, he raised it in the air.

'To our complete control of Deaf Smith County,' he said.

'But, Boss, your glass ain't got nothin' in it?'

'I am well aware of that fact, Dude, but, unfortunately, I promised Melinda I would stop drinking. If she caught me, she would raise Old Ned.'

Dude smiled and turned up his glass, sucking down the expensive double malt beverage. He was about to ask for another when Melinda sashayed into the office.

She went straight to her father's side. 'Father, do I smell alcohol?' Her tone bordered on indignant. 'Are you breaking your promise to me?'

'No, my nosey daughter, I am not. I gave Dude a drink in celebration of a business deal, and now he is leaving.'

Dude took the hint and backed out of the office, closing the door behind him.

'A business deal, Daddy. Is it a good one?'

'Melinda, by this time next week we will be the sole owners of the Double-A-Slash ranch.'

'Oh, Daddy that is the best news, and without a fight. I am so pleased, and, of course relieved. How did you get that stubborn Mr Bale Armstrong to agree to sell without a struggle? No fighting, right Father?'

'Why, Melinda, you hurt me to the quick. I would never do a thing to force Mr Armstrong off of his land. You listen to too much gossip. Now go home early today and get all dressed up. We will go to the hotel dining room and celebrate with a fancy dinner.'

'Wonderful, Father. I will finish up and go right away.' Melinda Quarry flew from the office.

Mort Quarry looked at his empty glass and sighed. He put it and the bottle of Scotch back into the cabinet and locked the small door. 'No warm Scotch today, perhaps,' he said, rubbing his lips, 'but we will have chilled champagne tonight.'

12

As Jim rode into Two Bucks City for the night, he tried to think about what he would do tomorrow, but his mind wouldn't co-operate. The bonk on the skull had caused his head to hurt all day, tiring him out quicker than usual. He decided to grab a quick bite at the hotel restaurant and then go to bed.

Jim trotted his mare into town and set her up at the livery. He walked to the hotel, going to his room just long enough to wash up and put on a clean shirt for supper. Most of the time it made little difference to Jim how he looked when it came time to eat. Tonight for some reason he felt like he ought to look a little bit more presentable than normal. He pulled on a sky blue shirt with black buttons in a horseshoe shape on the front. He extra-washed his face and ears and slicked down his long black hair with his fingers. Ready, he stepped out into the hallway and headed for the stairs.

Jim followed the aroma of food into the bustling dining room. White shirted waiters scurried about the place. Jim chose a table that sat out of the way in a front corner. He straddled a chair, facing his back to the wall. The waiter brought a menu, but Jim didn't look at it. He ordered beefsteak rare, beans, potatoes and coffee, the blacker the better. The waiter was right back with the coffee. Jim thanked him and sat back in his chair to sip the burning brew and watch the other diners.

The Quarry Hotel dining room had a far reaching reputation for good food and immaculate service. People from six counties came to town just to dine at the prestigious restaurant. Jim had to admit that whatever Quarry was, he did go first class. Too bad he was a low down thief. He sat back and as the coffee and the nice soft chair began to take effect, Jim felt the knots and kinks in his muscles begin to melt away. In spite of the bad day he had experienced, he was beginning to feel pretty good. His eyes were almost closed when he heard the voice of an angel. He jerked his eyelids open and realized the golden voice was standing beside his table and was directed towards him.

'Father,' said Melissa, 'This is Jim, er, Mr Butler, our new depositor.'

Jim jumped up from his seat like he had been hot footed.

'Mr Butler, this is my father, Morton Quarry.'

'Pleased to meet you, Mr Butler.'

Jim reached out and shook the gargantuan paw that was extended to him. His hand disappeared up to the wrist inside the large man's hand. 'Howdy,' Jim managed to squeak out.

'Mr Butler, if you are dining alone, we would be pleased if you would join us for dinner,' said the angel. 'We are celebrating an important acquisition to our family of businesses.'

Mort Quarry's eyes betrayed his

surprise at his daughter's invitation to this stranger, but his attitude remained cordial. 'Melissa, forgive me for saying this, but I believe Mr Butler has had a long hard day and might prefer to dine alone tonight. Isn't that so, Mr Butler?'

Jim nodded in agreement, excusing himself from their celebration for the exact reasons Mort Quarry had stated. Melissa expressed mild disappointment, and she and her father went off to a private room in the back of the restaurant.

Jim wondered offhand how Quarry knew so much about his hard day, then it came to him. Val Rose must have already told him about the incident at the Double-A-Slash. How much did Quarry really know? He had no way of knowing Jim was Bale Armstrong Jr. Or did he? Jim's thoughts were interrupted by the waiter bringing his food. With no more thought of his problems, Jim attacked the steak and fixings like he had never eaten before. He was half way through wolfing the meal down when Mort Quarry approached his table. Dude Miller and two other men stood around the giant banker looking like they were guarding some sort of valuable treasure. As the men spread loosely away from Quarry, Jim realized that the one in the back was Cormac McCafferty, the Irish Kid. The Kid stood stone faced and evil looking. Jim grinned inside as he thought how two could play the game of spying.

He looked up at Mort Quarry with a puzzled look on his face. 'What can I do for you, Mr Quarry?'

Both of Jim's hands were under the table, a fact that did not go unnoticed by Dude Miller. He fidgeted around and his fingers twitched as his boss spoke.

'Mr Butler, I know who you are, and I know why you are here.'

Jim swallowed, involuntarily, but otherwise showed no reaction to Mort Quarry's statement.

'I know you are supposed to be a quick man with a gun, but I also know you crawfished the other night rather than face Mr McCafferty, here. Well, Mr Butler, the Irish Kid is in my employ now, and he will be more than willing to meet you at your convenience to determine who is the faster gun. If that is too much for you, sir, then let me suggest an alternative. You ride out of Two Bucks City first thing in the morning and don't look back. Your job is finished with Bale Armstrong. You have failed at your task. Within the week, I will be the sole proprietor of the Double-A-Slash ranch. Bale Armstrong is a beaten man.'

Jim's insides churned to the boiling point. He was ready to face up to who he was and to let it be known what would happen to Mr Mort Quarry and his gunslicks if they even set foot on his father's ranch. His hand closed on the pistol at his side. He glanced at the Irish Kid. The Kid moved into position to help his partner clean house. Jim started to speak when an intruder changed his plan.

'Daddy, the champagne is ready. The sommelier is waiting to remove the cork as we speak.' She looked down at Jim, who struggled to soften his features. He only managed a partial success. 'Mr Butler, are you sure you won't join us? The invitation is still open.'

'I'm sorry my dear, Mr Butler has made other arrangements for the rest of the evening. Please allow me to pay for your meal. It is the least I can do for our newest depositor. Come, Melissa, it is time to toast our great fortune. Dude, Hank, join us. Mr McCafferty, why don't you accompany Mr Butler and see that he gets his little chore taken care of.'

Quarry hooked Melissa's arm and they strolled back to their party. Melissa tried to look back, but her father's firm grasp prevented her from doing so. At the same time, the two bodyguards blocked her vision.

'All right, Butler, you heard the boss, let's skedaddle on up to that room of yours and get you squared away. We wouldn't want you to have to be gettin' ready in the mornin' and be dallyin' too long for your own good.' The Irish Kid's smile was pure malevolence. 'Of course, if you want to do it the other way and face me like a man.' The Kid said the last part way louder than he had to. People close to the two men stopped their conversations to see what might happen next. Jim scowled at the Kid but did nothing. He rose from his seat and, with the Irish Kid dogging his every step, trudged up to his room.

Jim unlocked the door and stepped inside his room. Cormac followed him in and closed the door. Jim walked over to the bed and removed his gun belt. He motioned the grinning Kid to step over to him. The Kid obliged. Jim stuck out his right hand, and the Kid reached to shake it. Jim clamped his fingers around Cormac's hand and with a lightning move jerked the Kid off balance. Jim's left hand shot around and connected to the unsuspecting man's jaw. The Irish Kid dropped like a horse apple.

Shaking his head to clear the cobwebs, Cormac peered up at Jim from a bulging right eye and a bloodshot left one.

'Cormac, you ever embarrass me again around a bunch of respectable people, we will go out behind a barn, and I will show you who the best *pistolero* is.'

Cormac McCarty looked up at Jim with innocent green eyes. 'Shucks, Jimmy,' he said, 'I expect that feller would be Wild Bill Hickok, wouldn't it?'

Jim Butler stared down at his compadre for a moment, and then both broke into raucous laughter.

13

'It wasn't a problem at all gettin' hired on with that bunch of polecats,' said the Irish Kid. 'I just charmed 'em with a little of the old Irish blarney, and they just naturally couldn't stand to do without me.' He dug a finger in his teeth, moseyed over to the window and spat out a tiny piece of beef. 'Ol' Mr Quarry, he lays out a doggone tasty spread of vittles for us workin' cowhands. It's gonna bother me a right smart to have to be shootin' some of them boys pretty soon.' He peered at Jim out of the corner of his eye.

'If you're through spouting off the wonderful qualities of your new boss, Cormac, maybe now we can get down to business. If you don't show back up at the party pretty soon, Quarry might send someone up to check on you.'

The Kid nodded and grabbed the

one chair in the room, spun it around backwards, and sat down straddle-legged.

'So far, Jimmy, all I know is that they're plannin' somethin' real big, real soon. Bein' new, I ain't been privy to no inside information.'

'Did you find out where they're keeping my brother?'

'Yep, that I did find out. They got him up at an old line shack way back in the hills, deep inside Quarry's ranch. That's somethin' else I was goin' to tell you. I got me a strong hunch that whatever it is they're gonna do, it involves your brother.'

Jim got up, walked to the window, and stared out. The night was as black as the devil's heart. A breeze drifted in from the north, cooling the dry air. The evening cacophony of street sounds was dying down. Two Bucks City was rolling up its sidewalks, ending another day.

★ ★ ★

Midnight had passed and the moonless night shrouded the country in cavernous shadows. Dude Miller and four other men rode up to the line shack where Chris Armstrong and Charley Pratt awaited the big orders from the boss. Dude was in charge, but all of the Quarry men had been instructed to act as if Chris were the head honcho. The five made their way to the dilapidated old cabin, dismounted and went inside.

All the men said their howdys to Charley and Chris, some even calling Chris 'boss'. The young man enjoyed the attention. He was ready for bigger things and he didn't intend to let Mr Quarry down. When his boss found out he could get the job done, Chris thought he might just set his eyes on that good looking Melissa Quarry. A man could do a lot worse than marry the beautiful daughter of the richest man in the panhandle. Chris couldn't help but smile.

'Looks like you're feelin' a heap better, Chris.' Dude strolled over and patted the boy on the back. 'You up to some hard ridin' tonight? When we pull this deal off, it will only be a matter of time before you're sittin' in that big old easy chair of your daddies out at the Double-A-Slash.'

'What's the plan, Dude?'

'No time to talk now, I'll fill you in on the way. Pete's got your horse saddled and ready to go, so let's vamoose.'

Dude took off leading the six men down a faint trail, headed in the direction of the Armstrong ranch. Despite the lack of light, the seven riders made good time in getting to where the Double-A-Slash herd was bedded down. Upon reaching the herd, Charley rode ahead while the remaining men stayed back in the trees. He cupped his hands and let out a long low whistle.

Val Rose, riding night guard, heard the whistle coming from the trees. He nudged his pony's sides and walked him in the direction of the sound. As he neared the trees, Charley called out to him.

'Val, it's me, Charley Pratt. Is everything hunkydory?'

'As well as it's gonna be,' answered Val. 'There's a new man on the other side of the herd named Bonner. He looks like a tough *hombre*, might cause us some trouble.'

'If he tries anything we'll make him wish he stayed on the farm,' said Charley.

'Now, Charley, Dude gave me his word there wouldn't be no killin' done here tonight. I can't be no part of somebody's death.'

'Give you his word, huh. Well, I reckon that's about as good as gold . . . fool's gold.'

At that moment, Dude and Chris rode up to the two men. Dude had informed Chris of the plan along the way. They were to stampede the big herd of his father's cattle that were grazing down closest to the ranch house. The plan wasn't to steal the cattle, but to spook them enough to wake up the Double-A-Slash crew and get them out on the range. Mr Quarry figured that if they did something every night, always at different times, the Armstrong punchers would eventually give up and leave the old man in a position where he had to sell because no one would ride for him.

The plan sort of made sense to Chris, but he knew all of those punchers. Most had been there a long time; they had watched him grow up. These men were his friends, and he knew they wouldn't quit and leave his father high and dry. All at once, Chris knew what he had to do. He was angry with his father, but they were still blood. He was an Armstrong and this was his home. He could not let Mort Quarry, Dude Miller, or anyone stampede this herd. When his brother had left so long ago the last thing he told Chris was to take care of the old man. He had to act and he had to do it now. Chris urged his horse up to where

131

Dude, Charley and Val Rose were talking.

'Dude,' said Chris, 'I need to talk to you.'

'Sure, Chris, you ready to get this fandango goin'?'

'No, Dude, I'm not.' Chris pulled his pistol and pointed it at Dude.

'Hey kid, what gives here? You changin' sides?'

'No, I'm just staying on the side I was always on. It just took me awhile to realize it, Dude. You and Charley and that other fella bunch up here where I can see all of you. Come on, do it. I will shoot the first one who even looks at me funny.'

The three men moved their horses close together.

'Chris, thank God, you're here,' said Val. 'I was out here ridin' night herd when these fellers rode up on me. They was tryin' to persuade me to join in with 'em when you showed up just in time. They might've killed me.'

'Val Rose, is that you?'

132

'Yes, sir, Boss, in the flesh. What are we gonna do with these here cattle rustlers?'

Chris was confused. He had known and trusted Valentine Rose for over five years, and had considered the man his best friend. He had to be telling the truth. Chris wasn't sure what to do, and he made a snap decision.

'OK, Val, I believe you,' said Chris. 'You gather up these two galoot's guns, right now. Dude, you tell the rest of the boys to just stay put back in the trees. Tell them we are working this thing out and it will take a little while. Do it now.' Chris rode up next to Dude and jabbed his pistol in the man's side. Dude did as he was told, and Val rounded up Dude and Charley's guns.

'Val, keep a sharp eye on these boys. I'm going to ride to the bunkhouse and roust out some men. On my way, I will tell the other night guard to ride over and help you. Can I trust you to do that?'

'Yes, sir, Boss, why I can't hardly wait

to watch these hardcases kicking and choking on the end of a rope.'

Chris nodded and started to ride in the direction of Hack Bonner. As soon as Chris turned his back, Dude Miller's hand shot out and grabbed his six-gun from the loose fingers of Val Rose. Before Val could shout a warning, Dude raised the pistol and fired one shot. The back of Chris Armstrong's head burst open like a dropped watermelon. His startled horse jumped and Chris's lifeless body leaned over sideways and slid to the ground. Val Rose came out of his stupor and tried to lift one of the guns in his hand. Another loud pop rang out. Val leaned back, and then fell forward, slumped over his saddle. Charley Pratt rode over and grasped his pistol from the dead puncher's hand. The shots had upset the cattle and they were getting ready to run. The sound of gunfire brought the rest of the Quarry men out of the trees.

'Quick, Pete, you and Cavanaugh pick up the kid's body and tie it to his horse. We'll run the cayuse with the boy's body on its back into the cattle when they stampede.'

The two men did as they were told and within minutes Chris's corpse was sitting more or less upright on his frightened mount.

'Yeehaw!' yelled Dude Miller, 'turn 'em loose boys, and let's get the heck out of here.' He whipped his hat into the rump of the horse carrying Chris's body. The animal took off like a scalded hog straight in amongst the jittery livestock. The rest of the Quarry bunch emptied their pistols into the air with whoops and hollers. Some of the cattle started to bolt and within seconds, the whole herd was running blindly into the darkness.

'This ought to stir the old man up!' Dude yelled above the thunderous sound of thousands of hoofs pounding into the hard pack prairie soil. 'Come on boys, let's make tracks. The whiskey's on Mort Quarry.'

14

'Sweet Mary and Joseph,' said Shank Halsey, 'I ain't never been a part of somethin' like that. How many of them chowder headed cows did we lose?'

'Rusty and a couple of the boys are still out checking.' It was Hack Bonner, who had just ridden up with a bunch of the hands. 'They ought to be in shortly.'

'Well, daylight ain't too far away,' said Shank. 'You fellers go on over to the cook shack. I'm sure cookie has got the coffee goin'. Hack, what happened out there?'

'I heard two shots, right together. The beeves started milling, and I had my hands full tryin' to calm 'em down. Then, all of a sudden you'd a thought there was a war goin' on. Somebody started shootin' and yellin' to beat the band. Them jug head cows took off and I was ridin' for my life. The shots were echoin', but they sounded like they came from Valentine's side of the herd. Say, have you seen that runt since this all started?'

'Naw, come to think of it, I haven't. Let's ride out and see what Rusty's found.'

In ten minutes the two men were at the site where the stampede had begun. Rusty was on his knees in the scrambled dirt. Something lay on the ground in front of him, but Hack and Shank couldn't make out what it was.

'What in tarnation is that thing you got there, Rusty?' said Shank, squinting to try and make out the mess on the ground. It looked like a pile of old dirty rags. As he moved closer, he realized the rags were covered in blood. 'What is it, Rusty?' he said again.

Rusty Puckett raised his head. Tears cascaded down his cheeks and splattered onto the dirt. 'It's Chris. This pile of rags is Chris Armstrong.'

'Naw, that can't be. Quarry's got Chris hid out up in the hills. Rusty, you're wrong.' Even as he said it, Shank knew Rusty was right. Although it was almost stomped to pieces by the rampaging cows, he could still recognize the hand-tooled English leather gun belt lying in the pile before him. Bale Armstrong had given the rig to his son on the boy's eighteenth birthday, and Chris never let the holster out of his sight. The pile on the ground had been a man, but now his own mother wouldn't recognize him.

Hack Bonner sat astride his horse, his jaw muscles clenched tight. He never knew this boy; only saw him once, and didn't like what he saw. But nobody deserved to die like this. When Jim found out, there wouldn't be a rock in Texas big enough to hide the snake that did this. Hack rolled his neck to loosen the fatigue he felt. He hadn't gotten any sleep last night, and he didn't expect to get any more for a long time. Turning his horse, he patted the animal on the neck and nudged his heels into the big bay's ribs.

'That wasn't the plan, but as long as it worked, I'll take the results.' Mort Quarry was enjoying a rasher of bacon with scrambled eggs and potatoes. He usually took breakfast at home, but this morning he ate in the hotel restaurant. Pleased with the report Dude had delivered, he dismissed his *segundo*, and leaned back to enjoy his second cup of coffee. In a few minutes he would stroll down to his office and put the final touches on the last proposal he would present to Bale Armstrong for purchase of the Double-A-Slash ranch. With his son dead, his hands spooked, and his gunfighter run out of town, even a stubborn old fool like Armstrong would see that it was futile to continue fighting.

Quarry wiped his lips and rose from his table. He felt better today than he had felt in a long time. As he stepped onto the sidewalk, his thoughts turned to Melissa and how he would explain why Mr Jim Butler had to leave Two Bucks City in such a hurry. He smiled at the thought of his child falling for a two-bit gunfighter, and a yellow one at that. 'No, my dear, I have much bigger plans for you,' he said, 'whether you like it or not.'

Stepping into his office, he watched Hack Bonner ride up to the hotel. 'I may have to turn the Irish Kid loose on that one too,' he said to himself, a little too loud.

'What did you say, Father?'

'Melissa, what are you doing in my office, so early?' She had caught him by surprise, so much like her mother used to. He regained his composure and smiled at his daughter. 'Melissa I have something to tell you. Please, sit down.'

★   ★   ★

Jim Butler sat on the edge of the bed and pulled on his boots. He needed to get to the ranch and try talking to his father again. This time he would have

Rusty and Shank to vouch for him. He stood up and had just buckled on his gun belt when someone began banging on his door. His .44 Colt jumped into his hand. 'Who is it?' he said, eyes narrowed on the door.

'It's me, Hack. Let me in, Jimmy.'

Jim crossed the room and, gun in hand, opened the door. Hack hurried inside. Jim locked the door behind the huge gunfighter. Something in Jim's boot hurt his foot. He motioned Hack to the chair, and he sat back down onto the bed and began removing the boot. Hack stood in the middle of the room, not moving toward the offered chair.

'Jimmy,' he said, as he removed his hat, 'there ain't no easy way to tell you this, but your brother has been killed.'

Jim dropped the boot he had been fiddling with. Mouth agape, his eyes rose to meet Hack's. He read the pain there and knew Hack was telling the truth. Jim closed his eyes and took a deep breath. 'What happened, Hack?'

While Hack Bonner told him the

story, Jim sat and looked at the floor. The part about how they recognized Chris caused Jim to drop his head to his hands and weep. When Hack finished, Jim stood and wobbled over to the wash stand. Hands shaking, he poured some tepid water into the basin. He lowered his head and splashed his face. Done, he toweled off and faced Hack. His eyes were red and bloodshot, but his tears were gone.

'The last time I cried was when mama died. I cried today, but I'm not gonna shed another tear as long as Mort Quarry and his bunch walk the earth.'

Hack nodded his head.

'Hack, did they find Chris's horse?' It hurt him to even say his brother's name.

'Nobody had found it when I left to ride into here.'

'Hack, one thing Chris could do better than any man I ever saw, even when he was a kid: that rascal could ride like he was stuck to the horse. I never saw him fall off. He was dead when that herd started, or they killed him while the cows were stampedin'.'

'Let's go get them Quarry men right now, Jimmy.'

'No, Hack, as much as I would like to do that, we can't. I don't want to kill Quarry. I want to break him, take away everything he has worked for and stolen. I want him to see it coming and know in his heart that he is powerless to do anything about it. Hack, I want you to go get Chris's remains and take them to Doc Withers. Tell Doc to see if he can find anything that would prove Chris was dead before the stampede. I was goin' to the ranch, but I believe I will stay in town for a while. Maybe I can learn something. Let me know as soon as the doc finds anything. I'll be around town.'

Hack nodded and was out the door. Jim walked out right behind him. He had to keep a straight face. He didn't want anyone to know that he knew about Chris's death. He wasn't hungry but he went downstairs into the hotel dining room anyway.

Sitting at his usual table, his back against the corner wall, Jim ordered bacon and eggs, and coffee. When the food came he tried to eat, but couldn't. He drank the coffee, though, four cups: hot, black, and strong. His thoughts centered on his dead brother. Why would anyone want Chris dead? He was brash and wild, but he was harmless, just an overgrown kid trying to be a man and not knowing how to do it. The only thing Jim could come up with was that Mort Quarry must have wanted Chris dead. He didn't do the deed, but he gave the order. An idea popped into Jim's head and he sprang up, laid some money on the table, and stepped outside.

Jim pushed his hat back on his head and strolled across the street to the bank like he didn't have a care in the world. When he got there he hopped up onto the plank sidewalk and stepped inside. Melissa Quarry was alone at the teller's cage. When Jim walked in, she looked up to issue a greeting. Upon recognizing who it was, she dropped her head and went back to her counting. Jim thought it strange that her attitude towards him had changed overnight.

'Howdy, Miss Melissa,' said Jim smiling. 'How are you today?'

'I am fine, under the circumstances, Mr Butler. I assume you are here to withdraw your money. I will get the form for you to sign. It will only take a moment, and then you can be on your way.'

'On my way? Just where am I going, Melissa?'

'Why back to New Mexico, or Arizona, or wherever it is you come from, Mr Butler. My father said . . . '

Jim interrupted her in mid-sentence. 'Oh, that thing with your father and the Irish Kid, why that was all just a big misunderstanding. Heck, Cormac, uh, that's the Kid's name, Cormac McCafferty, and I have been saddle pals for a coon's age. We was just sort of play actin' last night. All that stuff don't amount to a hill of beans.'

Melissa looked dazed. 'Well, Mr Butler,' she smiled up at him. 'In that case, I am glad that you decided to stay.'

'Yes, ma'am, me too, I kinda like it here. I might even decide to settle around these parts. There are an awful lot of pretty things to look at here in this country, and I reckon I'm lookin' at the most beautiful one of all right now.'

Melissa slapped her hand to her bosom. Her face glowed a striking crimson.

'As a matter of fact, Melissa, the reason I stopped by was to ask you if you would take a buckboard ride with me this evening. I thought we might drive up on one of these hills around here and watch the sunset. Will you go with me?'

'Yes I will, I mean, of course, I have to work in the bank until four o'clock. After that I will be free for the rest of the evening.'

'Good,' Jim said, putting his hat back

on his head. 'I will pick you up at seven. I'm looking forward to our evening together.' He turned and headed towards the door.

'I'll see you later ... Jim,' said Melissa.

15

'In all my years of practice, I've never seen a body so torn up.' Doc Withers drained the lukewarm coffee from his cup, and poured himself a fresh one. 'Hold out your hand, son.'

Hack Bonner offered his left hand. The doctor dropped a small chunk of lead into Hack's open palm. The gunfighter gazed down at the bullet, and squeezed it.

'Found it lodged in the boy's lower jaw. Someone shot him in the back of the head. It must have exploded his brain. He had to have died instantly; never knew what hit him.'

'At least that's something,' said Stretch Cassidy from the next room. He had one more day and the Doc was going to let him go back home.

'Yeah, ain't it though?' Hack opened his palm and stared down at the slug.

He stuck it in his shirt pocket and started for the door. 'Doc,' he said, 'Jimmy asked if you would take care that his brother's body gets to the mortician. He'll get with the man to make arrangements later.' The doctor nodded his head and Hack exited the building.

* * *

Melissa Quarry had closed the bank right on time. She hurried home, went straight to her room, and spent the next three hours preparing for her sunset ride. She changed clothes three times and combed her hair twice before she was happy with the way she looked. At 7 p.m. on the dot she skipped down the stairs, hitting every other step and sat down in the parlor to wait. Her father had not come home yet, but that was not unusual. He was often late and sometimes stayed at the hotel. Since her mother died, he had begun to spend more and more time away from home.

A soft knock at the door announced the arrival of her riding partner. Satisfied with her reflection in the hall mirror, she opened the door. Jim Butler stood on the porch, hat in hand. He gulped a mouthful of the warm evening air, coughed and sputtered.

'Jim, are you OK?' said Melissa. 'May I get you a glass of water?'

'No, no,' he said, waving that he was all right. 'It's just that I have never seen anything as beautiful as you are tonight. Melissa Quarry, you are stunning.'

Melissa radiated at Jim's compliments. 'Oh, Jim Butler, you are such a flatterer. I haven't done anything special tonight.'

'Whatever the case, you are the finest looking lady I have seen in a long time.'

'Just the finest in a long time,' she teased, 'not the finest ever.'

Jim blushed. 'Are you ready to go, Melissa?'

'Let me get my wrap. It gets cooler as the sun goes down.' She retrieved her shawl hanging on the hat rack by the door and joined Jim on the front porch. They boarded the buggy Jim had rented, he shook the reins, and the horse took off at a trot.

Jim and Melissa sat on opposite sides of the buggy seat all the way to the hill Jim had picked out to watch the sunset. He found a spot he liked and guided the horse over to it. Bunch grass grew in abundance in the area, so the animal had plenty to graze on. Jim jumped from the buggy seat and walked behind the rig. Rummaging around, he found a large wool blanket and spread the covering on a flat spot on the hillside. He then reached up and took Melissa's hand to help her to the ground. Jim wasn't sure, but for a moment he thought he felt Melissa squeeze his hand a bit harder than she had to. The time was around eight-thirty, so the couple had an hour before the sun started going down.

'Jim, we have been sitting here for five minutes now, and all you are doing is staring at me. I am doing all the talking. Jim, Jim, do you hear me?' She reached over and squeezed his arm, hard.

'Hey,' he responded, 'what's that for?'

'Jim Butler, I declare, you haven't heard a word I said.'

'Sorry Melissa.' Jim stroked his mustache. 'I was just wonderin' how a plug ugly like Mort Quarry could end up with the most beautiful girl in Texas as his daughter.'

'Oh, Jim, my goodness, can't you think of anything but how I look. I have brains, too. I can run Daddy's bank as well as he can, maybe better.'

'Oh, I'm sure of that, Melissa, and you're right, I need to think about something else besides your incredible beauty.'

'Good, what would like to talk about? I am well versed in the Arts. What do you think of William Shakespeare?'

'What do I think?' Jim smiled. 'Why, I think your mother must have been a beauty, too.'

Melissa elbowed Jim in the ribs, and

pushed him over on his side, pummeling him with her fists. He lay on his side protesting the mock beating he was receiving.

Finished with the playful punching of her beaten adversary, Melissa offered him her hand in assistance. As he was being pulled up, Jim felt, for sure this time, an extra strong squeeze from Melissa. This time he squeezed back.

They sat close to each other and talked as the west Texas sky turned into a kaleidoscope of ever changing colors. The sun dipped below the horizon, turning the sky silvery indigo. A hint of the coming spectacular show of stars began as random twinkling filled the heavens. Jim stared deep into Melissa's eyes. He reached out and took her into his arms. Her eyes were closed and her lips were wet and inviting. She raised her mouth to his and he turned away.

'What's the matter, Jim?' Her eyes were open and questioning. 'I thought . . .'

'I'm sorry, sweetheart. If I had my way I would take you in my arms and never let you go. I have never felt about a woman the way I feel about you. Melissa Quarry, I love you.'

'Jim, Jim, darling, I love you, too. I wasn't sure until tonight, but now I have no doubt about my love for you. If you feel the same way, why did you turn away?'

'Melissa, I haven't been exactly truthful with you. I said that incident with your father wasn't real, but it was. Your father was trying to run me out of town. He threatened to have me killed if I didn't go.'

'What! But why?'

'Your father wants the Double-A-Slash ranch and Bale Armstrong won't sell it to him. I'm determined not to let that happen.'

'Oh, Jim, you must be wrong. My father told me yesterday that Mr Armstrong had decided to sell the ranch to him. That's what we were celebrating last night.'

'Melissa, do you know why your father said that? It's because only two people stood between him and his taking Bale Armstrong's ranch away, Chris Armstrong and me. Your father thought he had me buffaloed, and Chris . . . Chris is dead.'

Melissa gasped and twisted her hand over her mouth. 'Chris, that sweet boy, is dead?'

'Somebody shot him in the back and threw his body into a herd of stampeding cows. The only way we recognized him was by his gun belt.' Jim choked up.

Melissa sobbed and put her head against Jim's chest. She cried for a long time, not noticing the tears falling into her hair from Jim's eyes. He gently stroked her neck and tried to soothe her.

'Jim,' she said, her voice on the verge of breaking. 'Who could have done such an evil thing?'

Jim yearned to tell her the truth about her father. He wanted to tell her who he really was, and that everything was going to be fine. He couldn't tell her anything more without jeopardizing the whole plan. He loved this woman more than anyone he had ever known, but he despised her father and what the man was trying to do to his family. His blood was Armstrong blood. The same blood as his brother's that now soaked the ground of the Armstrong ranch. If Jim did not succeed, the blood of his father and his own blood would join that of his brother. He had made a lot of tough decisions in his life, most of them affecting only him. What he did now would affect many people; some he despised, and some he loved.

'Jim,' said Melissa, her voice a whisper, 'You don't think my father was responsible for Chris Armstrong's death, do you?'

Jim was ready to burst inside. 'Sweetheart, I don't know for sure who was responsible. I know your father didn't kill Chris.' Jim hesitated too long before he spoke again.

'Jim Butler, you do think my father was involved. I can't believe this. I confessed my love to you, and now you are calling my father a murderer. Oh, my goodness.' The distraught young woman raised her hands to her face and began to cry again.

Jim reached out and touched her arm. She jerked the arm away, and then swung it forward slapping Jim hard across his left cheek. Just as quick as the crying began, it stopped. Melissa Quarry sprang to her feet.

'Jim Butler, take me home this instant. I will not stand here and let you accuse my father of some heinous crime. If you do not leave Two Bucks City tomorrow morning, I will tell my father what you have said tonight. And I promise you he will not be generous as to your fate.'

Jim was stunned by Melissa's behavior. Without thinking he reached for her hand to help her back into the buggy. She slapped his hand away and scrambled up by herself. Jim walked around the rig and climbed up beside her. He shook the reins and the horse started for home.

Fresh meat would have frozen solid had it rested between Jim and Melissa on the ride back into town. When Jim stopped the buggy in front of the Quarry home, he made no attempt to help Melissa down from the seat. She jumped off the buckboard and ran into the house. Jim sat like a statue, not watching her go. The slamming of the house's front door signaled him she was safe inside, safe from all the bad things that could happen to a body late on a dark west Texas night; safe from the knowledge that her father was the most evil man in the panhandle. Most of all, she was safe from her father's worst enemy, an enemy that loved her very much.

16

Jim had ridden out of Two Bucks City well before dawn. He sat astride the big steel dun mare on top of the knoll overlooking the ranch house and watched the first rays of the sun climb the horizon. He squinted as the bright ball of fire and gas rose above the far hills. Little sleep had come the night before and Jim was restless. Today he had to convince his father that his intentions were good. If the old man hated him, there was nothing he could do about it, but, for the Double-A-Slash to remain in Armstrong hands, his father had to listen to what Jim had to say. He rode down the knoll, but instead of going to the main house, he headed for the bunk house. This time he would take his friends with him.

Jim dismounted and stepped through the only door of the rough hewn log building. The men were awake and shuffling around the room. Most were dressed and ready to head for the cook shack and breakfast. Jim spied Shank and strolled over to him.

'Rusty, I know you didn't like that cuss,' Shank was holding forth on the subject of Val Rose, 'but he's dead and gone now, and it ain't polite to speak bad about the dead.'

'All I said, Mr Shank Halsey, was that the galoot was a no good polecat, and I, for one, don't miss his lyin' carcass one little bit.'

'Excuse me, boys, but what are you talkin' about?'

Shank and Rusty looked up to see Jim grinning down at them.

'Why, howdy, Badger,' said Shank. 'We didn't see you come in.'

'No, you two were jawin' so loud, it's a wonder anybody else in here could think.'

Both men looked at each other. His two oldest friends had been partners for over twenty years, and they couldn't have argued more if they had been married that long. Rusty started to protest, but Jim stopped him short.

'Boys,' said Jim, serious now, 'I want to try and get through to my daddy again. This time I want you two to go with me and vouch that I am Bale Armstrong Jr.'

Another old time Double-A-Slash hand, Jocko Lunt, was eavesdropping on the conversation and jumped a foot in the air when Jim said he was Bale Jr. The old puncher ambled over to Jim scratching the three day growth of gray whiskers scattered about his face. He walked up next to Jim and stared.

'Well, I'll be a prairie dog's uncle, you are Bale Armstrong Jr.' Jocko said. 'Howdy Badger. We thought you were dead a long time ago.' He stuck out his hand. 'Remember me, Jocko Lunt?'

Jim gave the old timer's hand a vigorous shake. 'Howdy, Jocko, how are you?'

'Mighty fine, now that you're here, son, mighty fine.'

Before anyone else could speak, Jocko started yelling to the other cowboys about who was in the bunkhouse. 'Say, all you ner-do-wells, come on over here and meet a real wampus cat on two legs, Bale Armstrong Jr. We always called him Badger because he was so tough, and he wouldn't never give up on nothin' if he thought he was right.'

Shank Halsey tried to stop Jocko from letting the cat out of the bag, but Jim seized his arm and held him back.

'It's OK,' said Jim. 'The time has come for everyone to know who I am.' He faced the men who had become quiet at Jocko's announcement. 'Boys, I have gone by the name Jim Butler for more years than I care to talk about. Whatever you might have heard about me is only half true, but I ain't gonna tell which half that is.'

The bunkhouse erupted with laughter. The crew of the Double-A-Slash needed someone with the brains to formulate a plan to save the ranch and the guts to get the job done. It didn't take a bunch of book learning to see that Jim Butler was that man.

'My real name is Bale Armstrong Jr. Those of you that were here when I left called me Badger. Now I answer to Jim, but Jim or Badger, either one is OK with me. Boys, I'll make this speech short and sweet. I have come home to help save this ranch from that thieving varmint, Mort Quarry and his gang of cutthroats. There is no doubt in my mind that they are responsible for my brother's death. Now, I know some of you hands aren't experienced fighters, and that's OK. I'm not asking you to shoot anybody. Just keep your eyes and ears open. If you notice anything irregular, find me or Shank or Rusty or Hack over there and let us know what you saw. This is war. I don't intend for it to last too long, and I don't intend to lose. If you don't like what I'm saying you can draw your pay, no questions asked. Anybody got anything to say?'

Jocko raised his hand. 'Shucks,

Badger,' he said, his grin revealing just six tobacco-stained teeth in his whole mouth, 'we was with you when you told the boys who you were.'

Jim turned to Shank. 'Well, old son, I guess it's about time we went to see my daddy. You boys stand around me so he doesn't cold cock me again.'

He wasn't smiling when he said it, either. Bale Armstrong Sr. was about as predictable as Texas weather, which wasn't predictable at all.

★ ★ ★

Melissa Quarry yawned and stretched her sore body. She wasn't used to sitting on the ground for such a long time as she had the previous night. She stood at the kitchen stove making toast on a new fangled toast making machine that had recently arrived from St Louis.

When the bread reached the desired shade of brown, Melissa opened the hinged wires with a pot holder and placed the two slices of bread on a plate. She was looking for the butter when she noticed her father outside the back door. He was in heated conversation with Dude Miller.

'Dude, are you absolutely positive about this?' Her daddy looked upset.

'Yes, sir, ain't no doubt about it. I seen the Armstrong boy's body with my own eyes. Mordecai Burns, the undertaker, showed it to me. He said Doc Withers told him he pulled a .45 slug out of the boy's head.'

'Somebody was smart enough to get the doctor to do an autopsy on the body. Now they know he didn't die in the stampede.'

'What are we gonna do, boss?'

Mort Quarry ran his thumb and index finger down his chin. 'Dude, I want you to round up the Irish Kid and a couple of other boys. After dark tonight, send them over to Dr Withers' office. I don't want the good doctor flapping his gums anymore about how the Armstrong boy died. Tell the Kid to silence the doctor for good.'

'What about old Mordecai? You want us to clean his plow, too?'

Mort thought for a minute. 'No, just put the fear of the devil in him.' He smiled. 'Doctors come a dime a dozen, but good morticians are hard to come by. And, besides, I believe the Armstrong bunch will be needing his services right soon.'

Dude nodded his head and sauntered away. Mort Quarry started to head for his office but changed his mind and reached for the knob to the kitchen door. His abrupt change of direction startled Melissa and she dropped the bowl of butter she held in her hand. The crockery bowl clattered to the floor shattering into a dozen pieces; butter flew everywhere.

'Oh, my!' she said.

Quarry opened the door just in time to see the bowl hit the hardwood floor. He jumped back barely missing being hit with flying butter. Melissa was on her knees picking up pieces of the bowl before he could speak.

'What on earth, child?' he said. 'How did this happen?' He wondered if his daughter had heard the conversation with his *segundo*. If she was eavesdropping, he would find out.

'Oh, Father, I was getting ready to butter my toast and it slipped from my hand. When I grabbed for it, I dropped the butter. I am so sorry.' Melissa scrambled around on her knees picking up the crockery shards.

Mort Quarry reached down and grasped his daughter's arm. His grip was firmer than it had to be as he lifted her to her feet. He held her by both arms and lowered his head until they were eye to eye.

'Melissa, I have a feeling you overheard my conversation with Dude.'

The frightened girl tried to protest, but Mort Quarry's grip was like iron.

'I will tell you this one time, young lady. Whatever I do, I do it for you. Do you understand me?'

She nodded her head in silence.

'Good, now, someday you will own

the largest Land and Cattle Empire in West Texas. That will be my legacy to you. I will do whatever it takes to make this happen. Some of the things I do, you may not comprehend for a while, but someday when you reap the rewards of my efforts you will understand. All I ask of you is your trust. Do you trust me to do the right thing?'

She nodded again.

'Sweetheart, do not speak to anyone about what you heard today. Is that clear?'

'Yes, Father.'

Mort Quarry released his grip on Melissa's arms and hugged her to his body. 'Oh, my darling, I knew you would understand. I love you very much.'

'I love you, Father,' she said.

17

Maria opened the door to find Jim Butler and his friends standing there. '*Señor* Armstrong,' she said, bowing her head. 'I have been expecting you.'

'How did you know I would be here today, Maria?' asked Jim.

'Shoot fire, Badger,' said Rusty, 'ain't much this lady don't know about. She's one of them *curanderas*. They say they talk to spirits, got the evil eye and such like that.'

Maria's brow furrowed as she cut her eyes toward the red-headed cowboy, who ducked his head and averted his eyes. She winked at Jim, reached out, and took his hand. Her flesh was so warm that Jim flinched from the touch. She led him and his men into the big sprawling kitchen. Bale Armstrong sat with his back to them drinking coffee.

'*Señor*, we have visitors,' said Maria,

pausing for a moment. 'Your son is here to see you again.'

Bale Armstrong whipped around and leaped to his feet. He was face to face with Jim before it sunk in, what Maria had meant. 'I thought I told you lyin' piece of trash to get off of my property.' The old man began a frantic search for his cane. Maria, still grasping Jim's hand, reached out with her other hand and grabbed hold of Jim's father's hand. Bale Sr. started to protest, but Maria held on tight. She took both of the men's hands and placed them one upon the other. Jim stood still. Bale Sr. continued to struggle, but couldn't shake loose from the Mexican woman's grip. Gradually his opposition to Maria's hold lessened. Bale Armstrong looked into the eyes of the man whose hand was touching his, and found Jim's gaze fixed upon him. All at once, he stopped struggling.

'Badger,' he said. 'Bale Jr., you're alive.' Then he fainted.

Rusty and Hack lifted Bale Sr. and

carried him to his bed. The rest followed, with Maria fetching water and some clean cloths.

'Your father must rest, *Señor* Bale. He is not a well man and the truth that you are alive and here at home has been a great shock to him. Even a *curandera* would need all of her powers to heal such a sick man.'

Jim squinted as he stepped outside into the bright sunlight. 'Boys,' he said to his three friends, 'we got us some hard riding to do. I'll tell you on the way what the plan is.'

★   ★   ★

Mort Quarry was concerned about how much Melissa might have heard of his conversation with Dude. He knew she wouldn't break his trust, but still it troubled him. He decided to take a ride up into the hills. Long rides alone always cleared his mind and helped him to think straight. Without telling anyone, he went down to the livery, saddled his favorite horse and took off for the countryside.

Many hours later, Mort stood under a thick leafy cottonwood tree and watched a storm roll in from the north. He had ridden all day, enjoying being outdoors. It had been a long time since he had ridden on his ranch property. He was proud of his land, his cattle, and the mansion he had built for his wife.

Sarah had been such a simple person. She had never liked the house, said it was too big and a waste of money. Mort smiled at the thought of Sarah and money. Frugality was a way of life for her, while Mort liked to spend freely. In their last argument she had said that she was sick and tired of his grandiose ways. Grandiose, her exact words. Mort hadn't realized she even knew what the word meant. That had been the last straw. Mort had known it was time to terminate his relationship with his wife. It had been easier than he expected. Now Melissa was the love of his life.

He looked up at the darkening sky. The leaves in the cottonwood above him had begun to whip like thousands of miniature green flags. The roar of the wind whistling through his ears invigorated him. He turned his face to the heavens and yelled out like he was speaking to God Almighty himself. 'I did it all for you, Melissa, I did it all for you.'

*   *   *

The riders had been on Quarry land for about fifteen minutes when Jim raised his hand for them to halt. They sat four abreast staring down at the Rancho Bonita complex. There was still enough daylight to make out the buildings. The main house was massive. It was built in the majestic style of the Old South. Four white pillars stood on the porch which ran the width of the house. Three bedrooms crossed the front of the second story, each with its own private balcony. Hanging baskets of multi-colored flowers, sea green ivies, and delicate looking ferns decorated the front porch.

The rest of the buildings consisted of a barn, bunkhouse, blacksmith's shop, and a smokehouse. Every building was painted bright white, even the pump house. The buildings were unusually close together.

'Whooee, I ain't ever seen a place this fancy before,' said Rusty.

'Yeah,' said Shank, 'and don't nobody live in that big house anymore either. Ever since Quarry's wife passed, him and his daughter have stayed in town.'

'How did his wife die?' asked Jim.

'She fell out of a carriage and broke her neck,' said Shank. 'It was an odd thing. No one was with her when it happened. Quarry had expected her in town, and when she didn't show up, he rode out to check on her. He's the one who found her dead.'

Jim took off his hat and ran his fingers through his hair. 'So boys, do you think we can do this? That storm yonder is gonna be right on top of us when we stampede those Quarry beeves across the ranch headquarters. It's not gonna be a picnic.'

'Aw, Badger, we can do this with our eyes closed, but there's somethin' I need to ask you.' Shank Halsey had ridden with a burr under his saddle ever since he learned of the plan. 'Badger, I know most of them punchers down there in the bunkhouse; shucks, I've even rode with one or another of 'em in the past. For the most part they're good men. They work Quarry's cattle, and they ride for the brand, but they ain't gunmen. They don't get involved with what goes on in Two Bucks City. They don't have no doin's with Quarry's bunch of gunnies. Son, will you let me ride down there and warn 'em to get out or face the consequences.'

Jim thought about it for a moment. 'Shank, you've got fifteen minutes before we start those beeves to running. That doesn't give you much time, but that's all you're gonna get. Tonight I'm sending Mort Quarry a message he won't soon forget.'

Shank nodded and took off towards the bunkhouse at a gallop. Jim and the others started east towards Quarry's largest herd of cattle.

18

'Shucks, Dude, I don't need no help takin' care of one old man.' The Irish Kid knew he wasn't going to kill Dr Withers, but he was unsure just what he was going to do. One thing he did not want was a bunch of Quarry's men with him when he went to the doctor's office. 'It'll be quieter and cause less of a ruckus if I go by myself.'

'Come on, Kid,' said Pete Allday. 'We just want to see you work. It would sort of be an honor to watch a shootist like you take care of business. Right, boys?'

The few men listening to the conversation voiced their agreement. Some of them, however, believed The Kid wasn't all he was cracked up to be. They hadn't seen him do anything since the boss hired him but strut around and brag about his prowess with a gun or with the ladies. Some of them hoped he would fail at this task.

'We'll go and clean up after this one man cyclone, Dude.' This came from a man named Quint Mullins.

Mullins had been a part of the Quarry bunch for almost a year. Most of the men considered him to be the best man with a gun in the gang, even quicker than Dude. Then the Irish Kid came along and stole his thunder. Mullins was ripe to see the Kid shown up as the four-flusher he was.

'I don't see a problem with a few of the boys going along to watch the fun,' said Dude Miller. 'Maybe, it'll stop some of the grumblin' about who is and who ain't a master gunfighter.' He stared at Quint Mullins the whole time he was speaking. 'Mullins, you go with the Kid. Pete, Andy, Carlos, you boys tag along, too. But there is one thing I will make doggone clear. The Kid does the killin'. After that, you boys can get rid of the body, and while you're at it, trash the place real good. Make it look like somebody was tryin' to rob the doc. Now, Kid, go on and get it over with.'

The Irish Kid sighed and headed out of the saloon in the direction of Doc Wither's office. His entourage followed close behind. He had no idea what he was going to do, but he knew, somehow, that these men with him could not leave the doctor's office alive.

The wind was picking up and blowing out of the north as the five men ambled down the street. Dust devils swirled about, and tumbleweeds bounded through the air like giant hollow balls of twine. A Blue Norther was coming, bringing hammering rains with it. Great frosty globules of water splattered onto the dust blown street as the Kid and his followers reached the doctor's office.

Doc Withers arose with a start when the bunch of disheveled men tromped into his office. Just as quick, he sat back down and placed his hands on his desk.

'What brings you boys in here on such a stormy night?' he said. 'If you're looking for shelter from the storm, I have a pot of coffee on the stove. You're sure welcome to some. Here, I'll get up and find you fellas some cups.'

'Shut up and stay sittin' down, old man,' said Quint Mullins. 'We might have us some of that coffee after we take care of your lyin' hide.'

'What are you talking about, young man? I am not a liar.'

'You was the one that told the undertaker Chris Armstrong was killed by a bullet to the head, not by them stampedin' cattle. Well, old timer, that was just a flat out lie, and we've come here to make sure you tell no more filthy stories about Mr Quarry.'

'Mr Quarry!' The doctor was looking straight at his mortality, and the odds weren't in his favor. 'Why, I never said a thing about who was responsible for that boy's death. I haven't a clue who shot him. Now you ruffians get out of here while you can, and I won't report this to the authorities.'

'We're Quarry men, Doc,' said Pete

Allday. 'We are the authorities.'

The obscene laughter of the gunmen put Doc Withers on edge, but he was a long way from being afraid. He had been through the War Between the States, and there wasn't much he hadn't seen.

The Kid took advantage of the jawing to edge closer to the Doc. By the time the conversation had just about played out, he was almost parallel to the seated man and facing the four gun hands.

'OK,' said the Kid, 'that's enough rattlin'. It's time to take care of business. I told you boys I didn't want you comin' with me, but y'all were too stupid to listen, now, I'm gonna have to kill you.'

Doc Wither's head jerked up like it was spring loaded.

'Dang it,' said Quint Mullins, 'I told you knuckle-heads he wasn't with us. There was somethin' fishy about him from the start. You're with that Butler feller, ain't you, Kid?'

'Me and him are like brothers,' said

the Irish Kid. 'You know, Mullins, you're not as dumb as you look. You might've had a pretty good future ahead of you. It's a shame I'm gonna have to end it tonight.'

'They's four of us, Kid, give it up,' said Pete. 'Quint's as fast as you, and me and Carlos are almost as fast as him. Andy ain't no slouch, either. You've got one chance, Kid. Why don't you walk out of here and ride while you still got time? Ain't no man alive that could beat four to one odds when it comes to gunplay.'

'How about four to two?'

The Quarry men looked up to see a sawed-off ten gauge Greener shotgun staring them in the faces. Stretch Cassidy had been asleep in the back when the men had barged in. He had quietly dressed and waited for the right moment to appear. No man likes to look down the barrel of a loaded shotgun. The four Quarry men began to squirm around like they were standing in the middle of a red ant bed.

'Hey, now Stretch,' said Pete, 'you just be careful with that Greener. We ain't fools. We'll back on out of here and let this sleepin' dog lie.'

'The devil we will,' said Quint Mullins under his breath, and he clawed for his six-shooter.

By the time Mullins cleared leather, the Irish Kid's pistol was spitting flame and death. Two holes popped open in Quint's chest. He stumbled backwards until he hit a wall, sliding down to the floor in a sitting position. At the same instant, Stretch triggered both barrels of the Greener. Pete Allday took the full force of the shotgun in his middle. There wasn't much left between his chest and his knees but a whole lot of daylight. Part of the shotgun blast tore into Andy's right arm, blowing his six-gun out of his hand. He screamed in pain and fell to his knees. Carlos managed to snap off a shot in the Kid's direction, but the slug flew high. The Irish Kid's next bullet blew out Carlos' heart. The Mexican gunman was dead before he hit the floor. In less than a minute, two men were dead, two were dying, and one more was wounded.

Cormac ejected the spent cartridges and reloaded fresh ones as he walked over to what was left of Quint Mullins. Mullins was looking at the tiny holes in the middle of his chest. He raised his head and stared into the Kid's eyes.

'I thought I could beat you,' Quint said. 'You really was as good as you said.'

Cormac shook his head. 'Some people got to learn things the hard way, Mullins.'

The doctor's office was a mess. It stank of gunpowder, blood and human waste. Carlos and Quint were dead, Pete was blown to pieces. Andy had stopped screaming. He lay on the floor shivering like he was freezing. He was in shock and he was bleeding to death from his shredded arm. Doc Withers had seen Stretch go down, and he was in the bedroom tending to the man's wounds. Stretch was cussing a blue streak.

'By durn, if that don't beat all,' said the wounded saloon owner. 'I got shot in the same place as before. I'll be a dad gum prairie dog's uncle if this ain't the dangdest thing that's ever happened to me. I'll swear.'

'Sounds like you've said about every swear word there is, already, Stretch.' Doc Withers was smiling. 'Now be still and let me clean this bullet hole. The slug went all the way through, so I don't think I'll have a problem patching you up again, but, son, you have got to stop getting shot.'

Stretch launched again into another cussing tirade, but he sat still enough to let the doctor work.

The Irish Kid looked Andy over to see if he had a chance to survive. If he did, there wasn't much a one armed man could do. Andy had quit shivering and lay still. The Kid figured the man was almost gone. 'So long, *amigo*,' he said. He had liked Andy. 'You were a good cowboy in the wrong place at the wrong time.'

19

The Irish Kid helped Doc Withers get Stretch back into bed. The lofty man protested some, but the adrenalin from the shootout had begun to wear off, and he was feeling the effects of his new wound. After Stretch was made comfortable, the two men walked back into the doctor's office.

'Care for some coffee, son,' said Doc, seeming oblivious to the ordeal that had just taken place.

'Uh, yeah, sure Doc,' answered the Kid, surprised at the casual tone of the medico's voice. 'What about these dead men? You want me to take care of the bodies?'

'No, sir, you leave 'em be, right where they are. After I drink me some of this black magic elixir I'm brewing, I will stroll on down to Mordecai Burns' house and tell him what happened.

He's the mortician, and he'll take care of removing the bodies.'

That sounded good to Cormac. He didn't like to kill unless he had to, and he sure didn't have any taste for taking care of the corpses afterwards. He accepted the hot black liquid from the doctor and raised the cup to his lips.

★　★　★

Mort Quarry had made it to Rancho Bonito in time to beat the storm. He sat in his expansive study and gazed down at the twelve year old bottle of Scotch whiskey that rested on a table beside him. He reached for the bottle, handling it as one would handle a newborn child. He put the crown of the whiskey bottle against the lip of a tall crystal goblet and poured the pale amber liquid down the side of the glass. He had sworn to his daughter that he wouldn't drink anymore, but he felt like having just one. It wouldn't hurt him to have a small glass of the Scotch nectar.

He raised the glass to his lips. 'Here's to you, Bale Armstrong, you old codger. Within a fortnight, I will have your land and all that comes with it.'

* * *

Jim reckoned Shank's fifteen minutes were up. He and his compadres raised their six-guns and fired into the air at the same time. The herd, already skittish from the approaching storm, took off at a dead run in the direction of the Quarry compound. The storm broke loose before the cattle had gotten a hundred yards.

The rain was coming down in sheets, and Jim Butler had lost sight of his companions. They had become separated right after the Norther hit. Jim was on the right flank of the herd riding for all he was worth. Visibility had been reduced to only a few yards, and Jim wanted to stop, but he feared the cattle would trample him and his horse. He kept riding and hoped for a break in the storm. All of a sudden, a rare bolt of ball lightning charged across the sky illuminating the whole horizon. The flash only lasted for an instant, but Jim could see a group of white structures a short distance ahead.

He dug his heels deep into his horse's sides, and leaned forward in the saddle. The blue mare reacted with a sudden burst of speed. The big horse was gaining ground on the herd's frantic leaders when a slingshot stab of lightning struck a giant blackjack tree directly in her path. The ancient oak splintered into a dozen airborne pieces. Jim stood up in his stirrups and yanked back hard on the reins. The mare was running flat out when Jim jerked her head back. She reared straight up in the air, her hoofs flailing at the black void in front of them. The panicking horse lost her balance and tumbled over backwards. Jim went flying through the air straight into the path of the storm maddened cattle. He hit the ground hard but rolled to his feet and came up running in the direction of his horse. The crazed beast had regained her footing and, before Jim could reach her, she took off into the night.

Jim almost panicked for a moment, but he didn't stop running. Regaining his wits, he began to frantically look about him, searching for a safe haven from the charging herd. A large chunk of the lightning-split tree lay right in his path. He leaped over the massive slab of wood and squirreled himself down behind it. The maddened cattle tramped around and over the log showering him with dirt and rocks. Jim Butler squeezed his eyes shut and for the first time in a long time he prayed.

★ ★ ★

As the violent thunderstorm intensified, Mort Quarry thought he was having a nightmare from which he couldn't awaken. He felt like he was in the middle of a raging tornado. His house began to vibrate; a plate glass window in the front living room shuddered and popped out of its frame like an overripe boil, shooting shards of glass in every direction. One of the flying shards hit Mort in the face, tearing a jagged three inch hole in his right cheek. Raising his hand to the gash in his face, he realized this was no bad dream.

Mort sprinted to the door just in time to see a thousand pound steer run head first into one of the thick oak columns that held up the massive balcony. The column held and the steer went down, disappearing beneath an enraged mass of hide and hoofs. Abject alarm masked the man's features as he realized that his cattle were stampeding through the Rancho Bonito compound. He knelt by the blown out window and watched in awe as the livestock rushed by his home.

As soon as the last bawling cow passed, Mort Quarry ran to his barn and saddled his horse. His world was unraveling, and, if he didn't do something quick to stop the decay, all of his hard earned gains would crumble around his feet.

★ ★ ★

'Hack! Shank! I found him,' hollered Rusty. The little puncher had dropped to his knees and was digging like an armadillo, trying to extract Jim Butler out from beneath a thick pile of rubble. 'Oh, my Lord,' he said, 'I think he's still alive.'

Both men jumped down and began to help with the excavation. Struggling, they pulled Jim from his hidey hole. Hack had grabbed his canteen as he dismounted and, as Shank elevated Jim's head, he poured a tiny amount of clean water into Jim's mouth.

Jim sputtered and choked on the liquid. He shook his head and squinted his eyes, staring up at his rescuers. 'You boys tryin' to drown me?' He said.

Tears ran down Rusty's cheeks, balling up in the dirt that caked his face, forming tiny streaks of mud.

Shank looked over at his old saddle mate and grimaced. 'Dang it, Rusty, I think you would bawl at your own funeral. Can you walk, Badger?'

'Yeah, I think I'm OK.' With Hack and Rusty's assistance, Jim struggled to his feet. He was covered in dirt and cow manure from head to toe, but everything seemed to be working OK. He was hurting, but he figured that came from being scrunched up under the fallen tree for too long.

'Shank,' said Jim, 'you and Rusty better hightail it on back to the Double-A-Slash before you're missed. I'm goin' to the hotel and get a bath. Hack, you ride into town and camp out at the saloon. Keep your ears open and your mind clear.'

'No whiskey?' Hack screwed his face up like he had just bitten into a sour apple.

'No more than two beers, either, Hack. We've all got be on the alert and ready for anything.'

The massive gunfighter shrugged his

shoulders and stepped into the saddle. He dug heels into his horse and was gone.

The drovers found Jim's horse wandering not too far from where they had dug their friend out from under the lightning scarred tree. Rusty handed the mare's reins to Jim, and he and Shank headed for the Double-A-Slash.

Jim rode down to the Rancho Bonito complex to check out the results of the stampede. All of the out buildings were damaged but still standing. The front windows had been blown out of the main ranch house and manure covered almost everything. Half a dozen dead cows lay about, trampled during the mad rush. Jim searched the bunk house and the ranch house but found no sign of human injury. Satisfied that no one was hurt during the stampede Jim turned the mare towards town. He was anxious to get out of his nasty clothes and into a tub full of hot soapy water.

20

Jim arrived at the hotel and headed around back to the public bath house. In a flash he was stripped and into a tub of clean hot water. It took a second tub of water before Jim got all of the dirt and manure scrubbed off of his body. Finally, dressed in clean clothes and revived from his ordeal, Jim felt pretty good as he started towards the bank.

He was in the middle of the street when he heard a man call out his name. He looked up to see a rider making a mad dash in his direction. Jim loosened the thong over his six-gun and crouched in anticipation. Relieved to see it was Cormac McCafferty, he relaxed and waited for his friend to reach him.

'Jim, you've got to get down to the Doc's office.' The Irish Kid had a grave look on his face.

'Why, what's the matter Cormac?'

'Hop on behind me, Jim. There's someone there who can explain it better than me.'

Jim grabbed the Kid's arm and swung up behind him. Before he could ask Cormac any more, the Kid jerked his horse around and took off in the direction of Doc Wither's place.

Mordecai Burns had taken the dead outlaws' bodies to the mortuary and the saloon swamper had just finished cleaning the blood off of the floor. The doctor was in the back room with Stretch Cassidy when Jim came rushing in the front door. Seeing Jim, both men walked into the front room. Hack and Melissa Quarry were already in the room.

'Melissa,' said Jim, 'what are you doing here?'

'Oh, Jim,' she cried, as she rushed into his arms. 'Darling, I am so sorry. I have been a blind fool.'

Jim looked down at the young

woman, dismay masking his features. 'What are you talking about, Melissa?'

She told him about overhearing the conversation between her father and Dude Miller. When she finished, Cormac filled Jim in with the details of the previous night's gun trouble. Jim listened in silence, his placid features failing to reveal the tempest tearing at his heart.

When Cormac was done, Jim turned and stared out the window for a long time. Suddenly a voice appeared in his head. He felt it rather than heard it, but somehow he knew it was real. The voice told him to get off of his backside and start acting like the man he was, Bale Armstrong Jr. Jim shook his head and looked around to see if anyone else had heard the voice. Hack was talking and the others were listening to him.

'I'm Bale Armstrong Jr.,' Jim said.

'Why, sure you are,' said the Irish Kid. 'Who says different?'

Jim ignored the Kid's response. He stood up and stretched his sore aching body. The physical pain he had been enduring just moments before was forgotten. It had been pushed away to some remote part of Jim's brain, stored away until the job he was compelled to do was finished. Walking over to Melissa, Jim bent down and kissed her cheek.

Turning back to face his friends, a look of total determination cloaked his face. 'Boys,' he said, 'Jim Butler died in a cattle stampede last night. He lived a rough life and he's gone. Bale Armstrong Jr. is back to stay, and I'm here to protect my birthright. Anyone who gets in my way will go down.'

Badger looked at his friends, and his lips parted into a thin mirthless smile.

★　★　★

Mort Quarry had arrived at his office before sunup and locked himself inside. He sat in the darkness and drank Scotch whiskey straight from the bottle. The fiery pale liquid helped to soothe his nerves and calm down the torrent of self-doubt that churned inside him.

Rancho Bonita, his shrine to his late wife, had almost been destroyed. Sheer dumb luck had caused him to escape death. Someone had to pay, and pay they would. He would get Dude Miller to round up all of his gun hands and blow Deaf Smith County apart if that's what it took. He would put out a bounty on Jim Butler, Hack Bonner, Bale Armstrong and the whole Double-A-Slash crew, even that Mexican witch. Soon, all of Deaf Smith County, Texas would belong to him.

He had sat alone in his office and drank half of the bottle, when he heard someone come in the front. My Melissa, he thought, always on time.

He reached over and clicked on his lamp. 'Come in, Melissa,' he said. 'I am in the back room. I worked all night on the Double-A-Slash proposition.'

'Boss, it's me, Dude Miller. Are you OK?'

'Oh, uh, Dude, why, of course, I'm

OK. Why shouldn't I be?'

'You sounded strange and you were calling me Melissa like you thought she was comin' in the door. You knew she was over at the doc's didn't you?'

'Good Lord, Dude, are you sure about that? I saw her just this morning, and she was fine.' The alcohol clouded Mort's mind and caused his thoughts to be sluggish. 'No, I guess it was yesterday when I last saw my daughter.' He hesitated as he spoke.

'She ain't the only one at the doc's, boss. Butler, Stretch Cassidy, Bonner and The Irish Kid are there, too.'

'I thought we sent the Irish Kid to kill the doctor?'

'Yeah, we did, but he double-crossed us and killed some of the boys.'

Dude told Mort Quarry the story of the gun battle as he had heard it third hand from Mordecai Burns. Quarry showed no emotion as he listened to the bad news.

When Dude finished, Mort Quarry erupted in a torrent of profanity,

slamming a beefy fist on his desk top.
'No doubt Melissa has told the doctor
and her new friends that I was the one
who ordered the Armstrong boy's
death. So be it. Dude, I want you to
round up as many of the men as you
can find and meet me here. We ride in
one hour. Bale Armstrong and anyone
else who gets in my way are dead.'

* * *

Badger Armstrong stepped out of the
relative comfort of the doctor's office
into the blistering Texas heat. He did
not feel the sun burning his skin, nor
the sweat that soaked his clothing. He
felt only one thing. Rage. Not wild
unrestrained seething fury, but rigid
controlled anger.

One man was responsible for the way
Badger felt. Mort Quarry had tried to
take everything from Badger that he
cared about. Now, he was going to take
away all that Quarry held dear.

The Double-A-Slash ranch had belonged

to the Armstrong family ever since Bale Armstrong, Shank Halsey, and a handful of other pioneers had ridden into Deaf Smith County and made the land theirs. Badger intended to keep what was his.

He looked up and down the main street of Two Bucks City and read the name of each business: Quarry Land and Cattle Company, Deaf Smith County Bank, proprietor, Mort Quarry, Two Bucks Mercantile, Mort Quarry, owner. The names on the signs made Badger's skin crawl. His shoulder muscles bunched up like knotted rope, and he moved his head in a circular motion trying to relieve some of the tension in his neck. Badger planned to end Mort Quarry's stranglehold on Deaf Smith County and, by all that was sacred, he swore he would end it today.

21

Against the protests of Doc Withers, Stretch Cassidy left the doctor's office and walked over to check on his business. The Golden Ace was half full, a considerable sized crowd for the time of day. Most of the Rancho Bonito cowboys were in the place. Half a dozen of Quarry's gun hands were there, too, lounging around at tables, playing cards and drinking. Stretch walked behind the counter and felt around under the bar top. A smile traversed his features as his hand found the back-up shotgun he always kept there.

Stretch spoke to his bartender, Max O'Hara, and the man left the saloon in a hurry. Stretch settled in behind the bar. As he began to wipe down the bar top, he noticed a stranger at the far end.

The stranger stood with his back to the crowd; whiskey, the good stuff, and a shot glass stood before him. He had an unkempt look about him. His clothes were dusty and ragged, and his hat was pulled down low in front, hiding his eyes. His right arm hung limp at his side. He wore a .36 Navy revolver belted horizontal, handle to the left, across his middle, and a .45 Colt Peacemaker slung low on his left side. When he took a drink, he would fill the shot glass, set the bottle down, and gulp the whiskey all in one swift movement.

Hack Bonner and the Irish Kid decided to stop at the Golden Ace to wet their whistles before Hack rode to the ranch to round up the Armstrong hands and bring them to town. They stepped through the swinging doors and looked around. The place turned quiet as a mausoleum. Hack cursed under his breath.

The Kid smiled and whispered to his compadre. 'Well, it's sure been nice knowin' you, boyo.'

Hack Bonner answered the Kid in a voice loud enough for all in the saloon to hear. 'I'll most likely die someday with my boots on, Kid, but today ain't that day.' He strode up to Stretch and ordered a cold beer.

Cormac McCafferty snickered and sauntered up beside his trail mate. The noise in the place began to grow in bits and pieces, and you could have bet money on the subject every conversation had turned to. Hack glanced at the man at the other end of the bar. There was a hint of recognition in his eyes.

'Kid,' said Hack, 'Put an eye on that dried up lookin' hombre down yonder at the end of the bar. You ever seen him before?'

The Irish Kid looked up from his beer and stared at the stranger, who stared right back at him. 'I don't recognize that bone bag directly, but I seen him plenty of times before.'

'How's that, Kid?'

'Not him, but his kind. He's got the mark of Cain on him. He's walkin' around, but he's more dead than alive.

He's lookin' for somebody in particular to kill.'

'Look at him, Kid, see how he don't use but one arm. By gosh, that's Ott Carlyle.'

'Dang, Hack, do you think so?'

'Yeah, it's him alright. I heard Jimmy speak of him plenty of times. The man wants one thing, and that's to kill Jim Butler.'

'I believe I'll waltz on down there and put the fear of God into him, Hack.' The Irish Kid finished his beer and hitched up his gun belt.

'Wait a minute,' said Hack. 'I got an idea. Stay here and back my play. We might just get out of here today in one piece, yet.' He stepped away from the bar and moseyed down in the direction of Ott Carlyle.

'Howdy, Carlyle,' said Hack.

Ott Carlyle's good hand dropped like a guillotine blade to rest on his Peacemaker. Without looking at Hack he spoke, his voice a rasping monotone.

'You seem to know me. How is it that

I don't know you?'

His head swiveled to meet Hack, eye to eye. Dark bloodshot orbs peered from under half-closed eyelids.

'We've never met, but I know you by reputation. My name's Hack Bonner and I ride with Jim Butler.'

Ott Carlyle turned his attention to his whiskey. 'I suppose you intend to kill me, Mr Bonner. If you know my story, then you know I can't be killed. Least ways, not by the likes of you.' He turned to face Hack again and took a long step backwards, his hand resting easy on the butt of the .45.

'That day may well come, Carlyle, but today I have a proposition for you.'

Ott Carlyle took in a long slow lungful of air, like a man swigging water after a hard day's work. He pursed his gray cracked lips and nodded one time.

'Practically all of these *hombres* in here work for Mort Quarry. Now Quarry don't like Jim Butler or anybody who rides with him. Most of these fellers are cowboys who ain't interested in a fight, but six or eight of 'em are hardcases on Quarry's payroll. Me and my friend over there,' Hack leaned his head in the direction of the Irish Kid, 'when we get ready to leave this saloon, those men are gonna call us out. If you throw in with us when we get ready to go, we just all might make it out of here alive.'

'What if I just stand over here and let all you bad men shoot each other to dog meat.'

'Well, Mr Carlyle, then my friend and I will have to kill you, and you won't ever get that chance at Jim Butler. You might shoot me, but my compadre there is the Irish Kid, and you ain't got a worm's chance on a fish hook of killin' him.'

Ott Carlyle shook his head and looked up at Hack Bonner. 'You boys about ready to vacate this place?'

'Yeah,' said Hack. 'I think our business is finished here.' He turned and started walking back to where Cormac McCafferty stood.

Ott Carlyle corked the bottle of whiskey and stuck it in his vest pocket. He scowled and fell into step behind Hack. When the two men reached the Irish Kid, all three of them spread out a few feet apart and turned to face the Quarry crew.

A hard expression swathed Hack's features as he glared at the group of men. 'My name's Hack Bonner and I ride for the Armstrong brand.' His voice carried the entire length of the saloon. All eyes turned to him. 'I reckon most of you boys know who this ring-tailed wampus cat on my left is, since he done killed some of your best gunnies.'

'Howdy, y'all,' said the Irish Kid, grinning like a kid skinny dipping in the old swimming hole.

'This pile of bones and skin on my right is Ott Carlyle, and he says he can't be killed. Now, I know most of you boys ain't gun handy; you just punch cows and ride for the brand. Well, if any of you got a hankerin' to head for healthier pastures, I believe this is the time to fork your bronc and ride.'

For a long moment nothing happened. A few heads began turning, followed by a smattering of nods. All at once, men started jumping up and a grand exodus of cowboys took place. Within seconds the Quarry outfit was down to eight men. Charley Pratt was one of the Quarry bunch that was still around. He whispered in the ear of the man next to him. 'I'm goin' for Dude, you fellers hold 'em off 'til I get back.'

Hack drew a long black cigar from his shirt pocket. He rolled it around on his tongue, and then stuck it in his mouth. Digging a quirly from his vest, he thumb-struck the fire stick and, with cupped hands, lit the cigar. Hack held the match upside down out in front of him letting the fire lick at his fingertips. The match burned upwards engulfing his fingers in flame. Hack never looked at the match. The stick burned into black ash, and fell to the floor.

'It looks like we got seven of you left,' Hack said, blowing a great puff of smoke. 'I recognize some of you. Y'all know you can't beat me on your best day, and I ain't near as good as the Kid. Plus we got one more gun on our side and he's a stone cold killer.' Hack puffed again, blowing a huge cloud of smoke in the direction of the Quarry hired guns.

The Quarry bunch were not cowards by nature, but they were, in their own way, businessmen who were paid to use their guns. To most of them this did not look like a money-paying proposition. The tension was as thick as raw cane sorghum, and sweat poured off of the men like waterfalls. Somebody had to make a move.

'By the saints, that's enough.' Stretch Cassidy stood at the bar, a little ways away from everyone so he could see the whole crowd. 'I have gotten shot twice in these last few days and I killed a feller yesterday. I'm tired and sore and just about as mad as a man can get. I want all of you yahoos out of my saloon right now. You might think an old scattergun like this won't do much damage at this range, but this one is filled with double ought buckshot and it will take out some eyes, ears, and such. Plus, while you nitwits were jawin', I sent my bartender over to the doc's office to fetch my other shotgun. He's outside the door right now ready to come in blastin' if he even so much as hears a mouse sneeze.'

The sight of two short barrels peeking through the swinging doors gave credence to what Stretch had just said.

'Bonner, you and yours back out of here now. Don't stop until you get across the street. When they're gone, then the rest of you can go.'

Hack, the Kid, and Carlyle wasted no time in backing out of the saloon and hurrying across the street. The bartender gave the word and the Quarry gunmen backed out of the saloon in single file. When they were all gone, Max O'Hara, the bartender, a man as Irish as the day is long, stepped inside and sauntered over to his boss.

'Well, there, Stretch, me lad, I reckon we showed those ruffians who can and who can't. Reminds me of the time I stared down those Indians back in '68.'

'What does this have to do with an Indian fight?' said Stretch, leaning against the bar and gulping deep breaths.

'Well, me boy,' said O'Hara, twisting the end of his thick red moustache, 'on that day, I had no bullets in my gun, either.'

22

Badger had been lounging in front of the hotel collecting his thoughts, when he saw Max O'Hara sprint from the saloon into the doctor's office. He started towards the doc's, but had only taken a few steps when O'Hara burst back out of the office carrying Stretch's shotgun. Badger watched as the bartender ran up to the saloon doors and stopped.

Easing across the street, Badger worked his way close enough to the Golden Ace to hear what was going on inside. He was standing ready to join the ball when Stretch took control of the situation. When Hack and the other two advanced across the street, Badger trotted over to join them.

Jim approached Hack and Cormac. He gave the third man a cursory glance but did not recognize him. 'Hack, what happened?'

Ott Carlyle's hand went to his front holster. It was empty. The side holster, likewise, held no pistol. His head jerked around searching for his six-guns. He found the weapons sticking in the Irish Kid's gun belt. He showed no expression as he looked at the Kid's smiling face, but his eyes glared what was on his mind. Cormac winked at him.

'We almost got our bacon fried, Jimmy, boy, but thanks to your old friend here, we still got our scalps.'

'My friend, Hack?' For the first time, Badger got a good look at the walking cadaver. 'I don't believe I know this man, but I sure thank you, amigo, for helpin' my compadres out of a jam.' Badger stuck his hand out to the man.

'Has it been so long that you don't remember me, Butler? I might have changed a little, but one thing hasn't changed at all.' Carlyle turned to his side showing Badger his lame arm.

Badger gaped at the man, as

realization struck him. 'Ott Carlyle? You're Ott Carlyle? Good Lord, man, what happened to you?'

Carlyle's lips split into a mirthless grin. 'I've been chasing you ever since I recovered from my gun shot wounds.' He looked down at his lifeless arm. 'A man doesn't need a whole lot to survive on when he's got hate keeping him going. All I could think about for all these years was finding you and killing you on the spot.'

Badger tensed up. 'Why didn't you make your play when I walked up?'

'Because this grinning baboon here took my pistols.'

Badger and Hack looked at the Irish Kid. Cormac rubbed the butt of Carlyle's guns and winked again.

The Quarry gunmen began to spill out of the Golden Ace. At the same time, Dude Miller showed up with Charlie Pratt in tow, as well as four more gunslicks. Miller went straight to the men in front of the saloon and began to palaver with them. After a few moments, he turned towards Badger and the others. Miller started across the street at a slow walk. The other twelve Quarry gunfighters spread out in a semi-circle around the Armstrong group. Charlie Pratt was not among them.

'Are you a man of your word, Ott?' asked Badger.

'Yeah, why?'

'If we give you your guns back, will you swear to not try and kill me until this brouhaha is over with?'

'Doesn't look like I have a choice? I'll lay off of you until this thing is done, but if I live through it, all bets are off.'

'Give him his guns, Cormac,' Jim said, and he started walking towards Dude Miller.

The Kid handed Ott Carlyle the pistols, barrels first. This time he didn't wink. Carlyle took the guns, spun the chambers checking for cartridges and holstered the weapons. All three men spread out behind Badger and stood loose.

In the meantime, Charley Pratt had snuck around behind the saloon and entered the place through the back entry way. He sneaked through the store room until he reached the door leading into the bar. Edging the door open he could see Stretch Cassidy and his bartender peering over the swinging doors, shotguns in hand. Charley crept up to within a few feet of the two men.

'Boys, drop them shotguns,' said Charley, through clenched teeth, 'and do it real easy like. I'd plumb hate it if we lost both of our bartenders at the same time.'

Charley sauntered up closer to the door so he could be heard outside. 'Dude,' he yelled. 'Everything is hunky dory in the saloon. These boys are quiet as church mice.' He laughed again, and prodded Stretch Cassidy on his injured shoulder with the barrel of his six-gun.

The saloon owner yelled and dropped to his knees. Max O'Hara twisted around to face Charley and got a rap on his head for the effort. O'Hara staggered back against the wall, but he didn't go down.

'Be still and shut up,' said Charley.

'Miller, this is between me and you,' said Badger. 'Let's leave everybody else out of it. We go head to head. One of us dies; the other rides out of Two Bucks City forever.'

'What makes you think I will leave after I kill you, Butler?'

'My name ain't Butler, it's Bale Armstrong Jr., and I'll take your word on leavin'.'

'My word, why sure, I'll give you my word, and it don't make no difference who you are, I'm going to kill you anyway.' Dude raised his voice so all could hear him. 'Quarry men, listen up, if this hombre kills me, you boys go on back in the saloon and have a drink in my honor. Mr Quarry has about run his string out here in this country, anyway, and it's time you hardcases drifted.'

'Watch yourselves, boys,' Badger said to his men. 'There ain't no honor on this street, today.'

* * *

Mort Quarry had heard the commotion and stood just inside his office with the door cracked. He could hear everything that was being said. 'How dare Dude say I'm through in Two Bucks City?' Quarry whispered to himself. 'If the Armstrong brat doesn't kill him, I will, and then I will take direct charge of my men. This county will be mine, yet.'

* * *

Badger Armstrong pursed his lips and breathed easy. He could feel the sun bearing down upon him and it felt good. He tasted the dust, blown up from a slight breeze. The particles mixed with the sweat pouring down his face, forming a salty gray paste at the corners of his mouth. Salty, thought Badger. He hoped he was still alive to enjoy the simple pleasures of life when this was done.

'We ain't got all day, Miller, pull iron or leave town.'

'Well, Armstrong, I been thinking about that.' Dude Miller's eyes narrowed. 'Maybe, we could talk this out. What do you think?' Miller blinked and grabbed for his pistol. He fired before he was ready; the bullet flew wide.

Badger's draw was smooth, and his aim was accurate. His six-gun barked twice, and two finger-sized holes materialized on Dude Miller's shirt. Before the blood could flow from the wounds, Miller was face down in the street.

When the gunshots went off, Charley Pratt jumped like he had been hit by one of the rounds. He took his eyes off of Max O'Hara for an instant to see who had been shot. The big bartender slammed his right fist square into Charley Pratt's mouth. Pratt's front teeth shot out like bats leaving a cave.

The breeze had died, and the silence roared in Badger's ears. The count was still four guns to twelve, and none of the Quarry gunmen had shown any inclination to head inside the saloon. It was still bad odds for him and his bunch. All at once a man came running down the street. It was Mort Quarry, and he was yelling to beat the band.

'Hold it right there,' Quarry hollered. 'Don't let that murderer get away. Stop him.'

The Quarry gunslingers opened up and let their boss get through. He stopped in front of his men.

'We all saw what happened. The Armstrong boy shot and killed Dude Miller in cold blood. You'll hang for this, Armstrong. As the first citizen of Two Bucks City, I demand you hand your guns over to me. That goes for the rest of your gang, too. That man that's down, someone check on him. If he's alive get his weapons too.'

'Man down?' said Badger. He gave a quick look behind him to find the Irish Kid and Hack Bonner still standing.

Ott Carlyle was not so lucky. He was on the street sitting with his back to a watering trough. Blood leaked from just below his breastbone. Odd wheezing sounds escaped from his open mouth. His quest for Jim Butler was done.

Badger turned back to face Mort Quarry and his men. 'Quarry, you're finished in this county. I've sent for a Texas Ranger. He ought to be ridin' in here any day now. You have nothing left to fight for, Quarry. Your *segundo* is dead. Your cowhands have pulled up stakes, and what gunfighters you have left don't know whether to whittle or spit. Give it up, man.'

Mort Quarry's right hand shot inside his coat clutching for the .41 cal. Pocket pistol concealed there. The deafening blast of two twelve gauge shot guns being fired simultaneously, caused him to drop the revolver to the ground and duck for cover.

'That'll be enough of that,' said Shank Halsey, cracking a long-barreled twelve gauge Colt shotgun. He popped the empty shell casings out and reloaded in one deft movement. Beside him, Rusty Puckett did the same.

Behind the two Double-A-Slash riders rode a half dozen more. What they may have lacked in skill they more than compensated for with weaponry. Each man carried a shotgun or a rifle as well as a short gun.

Following close behind the riders was a wagon loaded down with Mexican farmers. Three people crowded the wagon seat. Maria held the reins, and Miguel sat opposite her. Between the two and holding on to them rode Bale Armstrong Sr.

Maria guided the wagon close to Badger and halted the horses. The Mexican men jumped from the wagon and formed a cordon around it. Each man was armed with a pitchfork or an axe.

Bale Armstrong looked straight at Mort Quarry. His voice was weak, but loud enough to be heard. 'Quarry, you took one of my sons away, but you brought one back to me, too.' He glanced at Badger, then back at Quarry.

'You stole my cattle, you threatened my hands, and you insulted my companion, Maria. I should kill you, but the West is changing. The time of the gun is almost over with. Men like you and me, we're history. I'll let the law take care of you.' he paused, looking at Maria and the Mexican farmers surrounding the wagon. 'No, we'll let the law take care of you. We'll hold you until the Rangers get here; then Two Bucks City will be done with you.'

Mort Quarry turned in a circle looking for someone to side with him. His gunmen were mounting their horses and riding away. The townspeople stood and watched, doing nothing. Each one turned their eyes away when Mort Quarry looked in their direction.

Quarry raised his hands and started walking towards Badger. 'Son, you beat me,' he said. 'I give up. You're the best man, today. Let me shake the hand of my conqueror; it's the least you can do.'

Badger glanced down at the offered

hand. It was a mistake. He caught the blur in his peripheral vision and dived backwards. Quarry's roundhouse left hook caught the brim of Badger's hat and sent it flying.

Jumping back caused Badger to lose his footing. Quarry jumped on him like a crazed maniac, stomping and kicking at Badger's ribs. Badger rolled up in a ball trying to lessen the blows. One well-placed kick struck pay dirt, cracking a rib and causing Badger to yell out. The pain was agonizing, and Badger quit moving.

Confident he had the Armstrong boy down for the count, Mort Quarry raised his foot to crush Badger's temple. When he did, Badger sprang from his balled up position driving his head flush into Mort Quarry's groin. The huge man grunted and dropped to his knees.

Badger scrambled to his feet and, in spite of the pain, began to throw wicked left hooks and whistling right crosses to the body of the kneeling man. Quarry was beaten, but still Badger pounded him. He grabbed the bloody man by the throat and drew back his right hand to hit him one more time. Melissa's face jumped into his mind and he turned loose of Mort Quarry. The banker's unconscious body leaned to one side and toppled into the dirt.

Epilogue

Badger sat on the edge of the bed as Doc Withers wrapped his cracked ribs. Hack and the Irish Kid stood to the side.

'I ain't sayin' that hombre don't deserve killin',' said the Kid, 'but your daddy was right. Let the law hang him.'

Badger winced every time the doctor wrapped the bandage around the cracked part of his ribs. 'My daddy,' he said. 'Who'd have thought it.'

Mort Quarry was locked up in a small room in the saloon. Double-A-Slash hands were to guard the prisoner twenty-four hours a day until the Rangers came for him. Charley Pratt, minus his front teeth, was willing to tell everything he knew about his ex-boss if it would save him from the gallows. Bale Sr. and Maria had gone back to the ranch to prepare a place for Badger.

Bale was still shaken by the return of his oldest son but, with Maria's persuasion, he was willing to give Badger a chance.

'Doc,' said Badger, 'What's gonna happen to Melissa?'

'Well, son,' said the doctor, his face stretching into a grin, 'why don't you ask her.'

Badger turned to see Melissa step in through the front door. He struggled off of the table and hobbled to her side. 'Melissa, are you OK?'

She nodded her head and hugged Badger. 'I'm hurting, but I will get over it. It's hard to believe what my father had become. I realize now that he wasn't the man I thought he was.'

'I'm sorry,' said Badger, not knowing what else to say.

'I have much to do to try and rectify what my father did. I have to start right away.'

As Melissa moved to exit the office, she turned and looked at Badger. 'I am going to need assistance in rebuilding my company's reputation. Will you consider helping me?'

Badger gave her his best possum grin. 'Anything you need, Melissa, just call on me.'

'Good,' she said. 'When your ribs heal, come see me. My ranch house is in dreadful condition and I am going to need a handyman to fix it up.' She closed the door and was gone.

Badger turned and looked at the doctor and his friends. All three had blank looks on their faces. So did he.

We do hope that you have enjoyed reading this large print book.

Did you know that all of our titles are available for purchase?

We publish a wide range of high quality large print books including:
Romances, Mysteries, Classics
General Fiction
Non Fiction and Westerns

Special interest titles available in large print are:
The Little Oxford Dictionary
Music Book, Song Book
Hymn Book, Service Book

Also available from us courtesy of Oxford University Press:
Young Readers' Dictionary
(large print edition)
Young Readers' Thesaurus
(large print edition)

For further information or a free brochure, please contact us at:
Ulverscroft Large Print Books Ltd.,
The Green, Bradgate Road, Anstey,
Leicester, LE7 7FU, England.
Tel: (00 44) **0116 236 4325**
Fax: (00 44) **0116 234 0205**

BADGE OF EVIL

Andrew Johnston

Lawyer Jack Langan left New York to travel out west to meet the father who had abandoned him. But he didn't expect to be offered the richest ranch in the territory — or imagine that he would be abducted. And he certainly could not have envisaged challenging the sheriff to a gunfight in front of an angry crowd of townspeople . . . For Langan to survive, he must discover his own courage and learn to understand the ways of the West.

BUZZARD'S BREED

David Bingley

When Jim Storme went to join his brother Red, and his cousin, Bart McGivern, in Wyoming, he was heading for trouble. Cattle barons were attacking lesser men, and branding them as rustlers ... Jim joined the cattlemen's mercenaries, but he changed sides when confronted by his brother, Red. When a wagon loaded with dynamite hit their ranch, it was one of many clashes between settlers and invaders in which the three Texans made their mark, and struggled to survive.

'LUCKY' MONTANA

Clayton Nash

Sean Rafferty wanted money to buy back the ruins of his family's estate in Ireland. He didn't care how he got that money or how many lives he ruined in the process ... A man called 'Lucky' Montana found that fate threw him into the deal. With a bounty hunter already stalking him, Montana now had to contend with Rafferty's murderous crew as well ... Now he must stride into battle, knowing that there is always a bullet waiting for him.